GUSTAVE GEFFROY

DECADENT TAPESTRIES

TRANSLATED BY
SHAWN GARRETT

THIS IS A SNUGGLY BOOK

ISBN: 978-1-64525-132-3

This book is dedicated to my good friend Olivier Nicolas, without whose help I would not have had the confidence to work in this field. A hard worker and dedicated father, he has given more to this volume, and previous ones, than will ever be known. We all hope to see him back on these shores again!

—The Translator

DECADENT TAPESTRIES

GUSTAVE GEFFROY (1855–1926) was a French man of letters primarily remembered today as an art critic and an early champion of the Impressionists, though he also wrote a significant amount of fiction. He contributed regularly to various newspapers, including *Gil Blas*, *Le Journal*, and *La Justice*. In 1908 he became director of the Manufacture des Gobelins tapestry factory. Among his art related writing are *Le Statuaire Rodin* (1889) and *Claude Monet* (1920). His works of fiction include *L'Apprentie* (1904) and *Hermine Gilquin* (1907).

SHAWN GARRETT is a freelance editor, critic and short fiction aficionado. He currently co-edits the horror fiction podcast *Pseudopod*. His translations include Robert Scheffer's *Prince Narcissus and Other Stories* (Snuggly Books, 2019), Gabriel Mourey's *Monada* (Snuggly Books, 2021), and Jean Printemps' *Whimsical Tales* (Snuggly Books, 2022).

CONTENTS

DECADENT TAPESTRIES

THE ENCOUNTER

(originally published as "La Rencontre" in
Gil Blas, October 29, 1892)

B ACK at home, the woman did not take
the time to change her costume, to take
off her veil, her hat, her coat, her gloves, her
boots. She went straight to her room, dismissed her people who were silently offering
their services, and dropped into an armchair
by the corner of her fireplace.

She was in the grip of the most violent
emotion she had ever experienced in her life:
she had seen, really seen, without doubt,
the man she could have loved, the man she
had loved since she was born into the life of
love—the one she had never seen before.

This time, it *was* really him, she was
sure. She had trembled when she saw him,
as at the sudden arrival of someone who we
have waited a long time for and for whom

we no longer hope. But alas, she also knew, immediately, that it was only "the stealthy apparition," which had occurred after so many anxious years, and which would never come back again. The length of the encounter had been just long enough for her to know of the existence of the one she had so eagerly desired, and long enough also for her to learn of the fading of his fugitive form, as rapid as its emergence.

This is what she was thinking of, with her doors closed, in that October twilight through which she had so feverishly returned home. Evening came, through the final violence of a cold sun. The blue and purple of the night already obscured the room where still shone, here and there like the last lights of life, the golden and pink reflections of the sunset. A dry gust from the northwest passed brutally through the gardens of the University Street. The few yellow and red leaves that had hitherto resisted, detached, swirled, and fell like dead butterflies.

This end of things, this death knell of nature that passed in the wind, this invasion of the shadow, this vanquished light, all conspired to turn her dreamy thoughts to a harmonious and funereal setting. She was in sympathy with the so very hostile outside world. In front of the barely pink fire, almost fallen to ashes, the woman had collapsed, thrown herself there as if into the bottom of an abyss. For someone entering, she would have been barely visible, her body indistinct and lost in the dark fabrics. Not even a glimmer of dying fire illuminated her fixed gaze under the half-fallen eyelids, the bitter corner of her mouth, her pale cheek resting on a hand gloved in black. Not long ago, when she had opened the door, she was tall, flexible, and her somewhat broken gait still displayed active life and potential energy. Now she lay, almost dissolved in the shadows, nothing more than a motionless, faded being who participated in the annihilation of autumn.

Yet she lived on, irrational and active, and pictured to herself, with cruel accuracy, the irony of her life. She repeated to herself with a concentrated rage—although she did not shudder and was rigid as a statue—that she felt born for love, that she was a creature of violent flesh and tender spirit, that she had hoped, since she was a woman, for the coming of the man similar to her and that she had always been mistaken in her desolate experiences. As a young girl, she had not seen the stranger to whom she was engaged approaching her. Married, she had known marriage only in its meaning as a social establishment. And whispering to herself her supreme confidences, she confessed to the disillusionment and wounds she had brought back from the fugitive searches which her despair of love had led. What! Had she lived only to record the nothingness of her senses, the bankruptcy of her imagination?

Yet, being close to the man this day, she had confessed to herself, by the particular electricity of the spirit, that she finally saw her inner phantom *living* before her. But it was over already, the real being had once again become, for her, a shadow without existence.

She remembered the incident of the meeting, the banal incident that had become so tragic for her.

During her return trip to Paris, two men had entered the compartment where she was, and immediately, at the mere sight of one of them, she had felt troubled, as she had never felt before. She had tried to reprimand herself, to reassure her being, but to no avail. She had wanted to analyze her sensation, to wonder why this newcomer, this passer-by who had sat by chance in front of her, had thus taken on such a mysterious influence. She had therefore looked at him with all the attention of her eyes, scrutinized him with all the strength of her investigation. But it had been impossible for her to tell herself what she felt moved by, both happy and desperate. She did not believe in witchcraft and philters, and the one who gave her this overexcitement had not practiced on her any formula of hypnotism, and moreover, she was very much master of herself, judging herself coldly and lucidly, although her discomfort increased.

She knew only one result, without being able to specify any cause, and that was that she was suddenly illuminated, from herself and the one she was looking at, by something that came from *within*, by all that is transmitted by a being's pace, attitude, gesture, movement of the body, and sound of a voice. Don't men constantly say that they suddenly fall in love, at the mere sight of a woman, and that, really, despite so many lies, this must have happened sometime? Yes, certainly, since we have seen loves thus begun, and they never end. Indeed, that's how it was for her, that's all. If love at first sight exists, this lightning had fallen now on her!

※

"So why," she said to herself, now that she had returned to her room and sadly sat by the fire, "why didn't I do what everything in me was screaming to do! Why didn't I tell the one I'd finally met that he was born for me, and that I was born for him? What force paralyzed my hands that wanted to take his, sealed my mouth that wanted to speak the words of my thought?

"Ah, no doubt I was imprisoned in habit, subjected in spite of myself to education, to the world, to my family, to everything around me, to all the people who know me.

"And then, also, practical reflections crossed my fevered mind, impossibilities were shown, the fear of ridicule, the fear of not being understood! This man I imagined, the man I was waiting for, the one I would have for me alone until my end, would have taken me for a madwoman or for a wanton woman, if I had only been able to stammer a little of the words that came from my heart!

"He didn't even see me. He constantly raised a low voice with his companion. I heard this voice at first without knowing what it was saying, and with the clear conviction that from now on I would always hear it. And then, when I saw that there was concern behind the words that came to me, I finally understood allusions to a change of existence, to a definitive departure. A few more days, and he will no longer be in Paris. He said the name of the hotel where he was staying, and that name, I know."

This time, she came out of her dream, she stood upright, in the shadows, her face whiter:

"Miserable woman! Cowardly heart, how can you hesitate? How do you not have the courage to try what a man in love would try with the woman he would love. But come now, go out, you will explain yourself, you will be understood, because you must finally be understood. Sacrifice everything that seems so oppressive, so heavy. The real truth is in this mirage you saw. There are no habits, no conventions, no society, there is your happiness that passes by, and you do not grasp it! You do not fall on this prey that will not return!"

All that can be repressed in life, a physiological revolt in a woman of today relaxed to hereditary mores and social conveniences, was agitated and fought in her.

She was, for a time, the battlefield occupied by the victorious instinct.

Her hands were shaking. She took a few energetic steps towards the door.

Then she stopped, stayed for a few moments without moving. The being of nature was slowly leaving, dismissed, defeated, to be replaced by the prudent socialite, who whispered:

"Yes, but... what if he was like the others—what if he was only the *appearance* of my desire!"

She sat down, listening again to the gusty wind, and watched the fire go out.

OLD EMPLOYEE
(originally published as "Vieil Employé" in *Gil Blas*, March 30, 1893)

IT would have been difficult to tell his age, although the habit had gradually become to call him "the old employee." He could have been really very old—or very young—and his quiet bearing, his indecisive countenance, furnished only the vaguest information as to his date of birth. It was known that he had been employed since the age of thirteen, and it was assumed that he was in his forties, going on fifty.

One thing that was difficult to understand, given his gray hair, his early beginnings and his regularity, was his low salary. He earned fourteen hundred francs a year—at the end of each month he received one hundred and sixteen francs and sixty-five cents.

Had bad luck always pursued this unfortunate man? Had he always lost his position when he was about to reap the benefit of long years of patient service? Had his bosses gone bankrupt? Had they restricted the number of their employees, and so had he always naturally found himself the first victim sacrificed in commercial and financial disasters? We didn't know. In any case, he earned fourteen hundred francs—like the newcomers, the young people among whom he found himself. As he was, poor, self-effacing, without activity and without protest, he was one of those who best brings out the mystery of life. This monotonous machine, his clockworks always re-wound, constantly accomplishing the same task; this human rag which had, in the swamp of an office, almost the same existence as those grayish larvae which one sometimes sees pass on shallow waters with a slow movement of boredom—in final point, this living man, so useless, so sweet and so sad, on contemplation could become infinitely mysterious and moving.

But this mystery and this emotion should not literarily be distorted, we should not contrive to highlight the hidden events and small facts whose interpretation would change his ignored existence into a visible drama. A being of this genus should retain on the printed page the same character, at once vague and precise or—rather—general, as the individual by which a species is defined in the catalogs of natural history. It should be enough to note its form, its passage and its vanishing.

The truth is that we knew nothing of his life, and we can believe that he too was not aware of his personal reality, of his momentary appearance among the infinite world, without beginning and without end, of phenomenon. Classified in this way, does he not take on an extraordinary type of significance, does he not command a legion of his fellows? An immense human crowd passes thus, by living the methodical, tranquil and vegetative life, without asking themselves if there is a how and a why to birth, to development and to death. Without asking if there is a purpose to the efforts, and a necessity in the willingly accepted moral and social rule. One can fix onto this one in question only fleeting memories: the distant image, the weak gait, the barely apparent wakefulness, traces of which remained for a little time, every day diminishing, in the spirit of some who were with him. And it turns out that these pale appearances, this barely perceptible glow under the ashes that accumulated over the years, is the summary of thousands and millions of similar souls. The obscure being who was born and who died without having had the sensation of the enigma of reality, alone represents the somnambulistic illusion of the immense majority of men.

Among those who had known him, those who remember describe him thusly: of medium height, with a round back, he seemed not to have reached his full development—his iron-gray hair was cut very close—on a slender, gnarled neck, his round head buffeted like a wrinkled apple forgotten at the end of a branch—the face was yellow, the eyes clear, innocent, childish, in deep cavities, the forehead wrinkled.

All of this was resolved into an expression of placidity, of unalterable calm, of rare speech that always equivocated. Sometimes the clear eye became clearer still, transparent like crystal and like water, absolutely childlike. The old employee then stopped working, his inner mechanism halted for a second, and he seemed willing to smile at thoughts which paid him a visit. But while he was almost smiling, he never did laugh.

He was dressed, at the office, in a black tunic, no doubt left over from the siege of Paris during which the old employee was obviously one of the "Thirty Cents." He carefully hung up this tunic every evening, with ends of the sleeves of a lustrine which he tied carefully every morning and which made him a kind of schoolboy like no one had ever seen before: calm and almost mute.

You never saw him without an umbrella either, and this concern for showers and squalls explained the state of preservation of his wide-brimmed top hat, a fashion ten years back. He wore only clothes of dark colors, the most economical, those which make even more modest and invisible the most humble of his kind, and he showed himself, in every detail, to be of perfect cleanliness.

At noon, he ate a little bread, and a bar of chocolate, and he drank a glass of water, never two. He was opposed to all excess.

This is all that was known of him during his life. He was astonishing at first, then pitiful, without anyone being able to say the precise reason for the feelings he aroused. He was the only one like that. How did he live, and especially for what and for whom did he live?

No one knew of any existence outside of his silence.

When in the evening, at seven o'clock, he went out, his long day of eleven consecutive hours over, and he went away, alone, without stopping, towards a distant dwelling, did he find a being who was waiting for him? A person of whom he thought during the day, who made him endure life with a little joy, with a little tenderness? Did he even know some harmless fellow like himself, with whom he could pass the evening in an almost deserted suburban cafe, in the smoke of a pipe, to the familiar sound of dominoes and billiard balls? No one knew, no one could tell if there was a single ray to warm the poor wizened being, so sweet, so self-effacing.

One day he left at two o'clock, ill, unsteady. The next day, in the office, someone said:

"He is dead."

There was a general surprise as a crowd gathered with strained necks and questioning faces.

"He died in the hospital, from a stroke to the brain."

A stroke to the brain! What had occurred to that tranquil face?

It was then learned that he left behind a five-year-old boy. This little one had fallen ill.

The father, at the office, overwhelmed by instinct, eaten away by anxiety, could hold it no longer, his peaceful organism disintegrated: fever seized him, then death. The little five-year-old boy will retain only a faint memory of the old employee whom he saw returning in the evening, his cotton umbrella under his arm, and under the wide-brimmed hat, his gray face lit up by his tender eyes and an attempt at a smile.

This solved the mystery, though we do not know what adventure the child originated from, what woman had passed through the existence of the old man, what chance inheritance he had accepted. They put this almost anonymous man in the common grave, and that, in short, did not change much in his destiny, because it was also in a common grave that he had timidly, silently lived.

THE FEELING OF THE IMPOSSIBLE

(originally published as "Le sentiment de l'impossible" in *Gil Blas*, January 19, 1893)

THE young girl who inherited the house of Aunt Clementine settled there with her family towards the end of the stormy summer. It was in a small town in Old France that had become a kind of large hamlet built of silent mansions, where the pavement of the streets was broken by grass. She had immediately liked the appearance of the house: the facade on the street, the beautiful Louis XIV windows, a door raised on a stoop of worn marble, the narrow courtyard inside overrun with jasmine, the tiny pavilion set back at the bottom of the garden. Similarly, she had made a full inventory of all the charming rooms, had learned again the history of her family from the portraits which smiled and gazed at the walls in their dusty gold frames, from the intact furniture guarded decade after decade, as if the missing might come back and find their familiar objects.

In the living room (the only really big room in the house), and in all the other bedrooms, big and small, whose spaces were decorated with bleached and faded hangings, the melancholic girl tried to relive the hours that had passed away, sitting in the massive armchairs, in the softly curved shepherds' seats, on rigid sofas. She scanned the tightly closed cupboards and fat dressers of rare woods, with copper locks and handles, but found them looking like tombs, sarcophagi, the well-closed vaults of the dead.

She kept a respectful fear of all the secrets contained in this house, as she had touched the old pianos and aged spinets and heard their whispers and complaints in frail voices. She felt surrounded by memories and advice, of possible reproaches as well, and was in communication with the unknown, living in an atmosphere of secrecy.

So she did not dare to turn all the keys at once, open all the furniture's doors and drawers, and took pleasure in delaying the moment when she would, with fevered brow and beating heart, disturb and evaporate the silence, perfumes and confidences of former times.

And until now, an invincible force brought her back every day—for most of the day—anxious and preoccupied to the same room, the second on the third floor, under the attic: a room slightly paneled, without much furniture beside a narrow bed, a chest of drawers, a dresser, a country cupboard, a little secretary that was folded down into a writing table, an armchair and another chair. In front of the bed was a small carpet, as narrow as the bed. In one corner, a door opened to a bathroom where clothes were hung. They were the strict quarters of a young man, a student on vacation.

But to the small and melancholy young girl this room, a little cold with its red waxed pane, felt like the warmest and most mysterious of all, the most inhabited.

A portrait above the fireplace filled the narrow space with a strange feeling of life.

It was the portrait of a young man, unpowdered, wearing a high-necked suit that appeared to be a costume of the time of the Revolution. He did not resemble any of the ancestors who instilled their bonhomie, gravity, and dead existence in other places of honor in the home. He did not have the appearance of an attorney, a notary or a soldier—lacking their expressions of quiet cunning and desired dignity of a comfortable family. Perhaps, by the cut of his face, the drawing of his cheeks, eyes and the mouth, he might have had a little resemblance to the women in the eighteenth -century toilets who hung in the salon in everlasting ceremonial reception—but he did not have their light glances, promising smiles of passing voluptuousness, and did not hold his head in their triumphant, ironic manner.

No doubt, this dead man, alone in this room, had been infused with a spirit.

He was not painted in the manner of the other portraits, with a care for the finery of the times, or its peculiarities. He was the only one of his kind, wrapped in shadows, appearing instantly unforgettable with his spectral color, closed lips, and pure eyes under a marble forehead. His face was pale, and yet a flame seemed to move on his flesh, burn his mouth, and flicker in the clear fire of his eyes.

Whenever the girl opened the door, some unknown reverberation of light animated this face and made her experience a strange disorder, becoming fixed with anxiety and a concern that was unlike her. Closing the door behind her, the shadows returning, she sat on the armchair by the fireplace, the young man resuming his countenance of concentrated sadness and serene gravity. Before this motionless dead man the living dared not move and so were passed hours of silent dialogue until the shadows of the twilight invaded, little by little, the walls, the furniture, and the portrait.

The little courtyard became all pink, the smell of jasmine rose thinner and warmer in the last heat. The visitor, then, slipped away gently on tiptoe and quietly shut the door, with a last look of timid sweetness at the face that blazed on the wall. With regret and fear she stopped on the stairs, almost at every step, her hand on her trembling throat as if she were coming back from a mysterious and dangerous rendezvous, and then she answered the call of her name and the gilding of lights.

There were many meetings like this during the end of summer, at every possible chance, a long reverie of love in front of this mute effigy, a delicious and dreadful season of confession to the reflection of a lover forever lost.

Her inheritance, then, was mainly the thought that she had found the only being that she could have loved, the one to whom she must fall by irresistible sympathy and sure affinities, but that he was exactly the one irretrievably far from her, dissolved in the funerary shadows.

For a long time, she did not want to know who he was, how he had lived, and what had become of him. Before opening drawers, searching for word of his existence with a trembling hand, she lingered in her ancestor's room recreating, with dancing and reverent figurines of Saxony and China, minuets on the consoles' marble.

Suddenly, one day, she decided to break the silence of the unknown man and an ardor of curiosity made her come to the room, shut herself in, and seek.

First of all there were books, books, and still more books in the big cabinet. Books whose titles and pages she wanted to read, all the literature and philosophy of the last two centuries, political pamphlets from the dawn of the revolution. Everywhere, interspersed between the pages, notes, and on the margins, more notes—fine writing, a little sickly perhaps, sentences of knowledge and generosity. He had a passionate soul and a high mind, the girl understood, feeling a thrill of pride.

In the drawers of the dresser were bundles of papers, plans for books, projects of social reorganization, letters (many signed with famous names), drawings, and landscapes. Not a woman's portrait: what a joy for the unhappy lover, widowed and jealous! But another portrait of the young man, a miniature made in full bloom of youth, in his eyes an air of seeking happiness and already, in the corners of the mouth, the bitterness of the future face.

She left it at that, that day. She found a name she then read in an old book of genealogies and memories kept by an Aunt Clementine. She discovered a removed cousin, an isolated indication. No wedding, no posterity. She ran the next day to the cemetery and found the grave. Died at twenty-eight. She came back infinitely tender and happy.

Until the end of the year holidays, she kept a habit of coming every day to spend her free time in that same cemetery alley. Her daydreaming about the past, his revived life, was divided between the room, where the eyes of the portrait shone, and the enclosed graveyard where wandered the invisible memory of the dead.

She left quickly and stealthy, as if for secret meetings, coming out of the house with light steps, a late lover who fastened the bridle of her hat, buttoned her gloves and unfurled her parasol. The main street was soon gone, and then the lane that led to the fields. It was there, very near, in the open fields of the plain that the yard, enclosed by walls and accessed by a metal gate, stood—the garden of the dead. An abandoned garden, where the wild growth of herbs and flowers unevenly covered the regularity of aisles at right angles, surrounding the graves. The yews and the cypresses shadowed the stones with their shades of crepe, ivy festooned them, and the boxwood framed them with dark greenery. And everywhere in this funerary scene blossomed roses, trapped in a lattice of thorns. They covered and perfumed the entire black garden, they assailed it with their profusion, hugged the trees, clinging to the walls and fences, falling to the ground like trailing fabrics.

The girl did not have the same desperate impression she felt in the big and gloomy cemeteries of the cities. With the light of the sun and color of the flowers, the idea of death lost its sinister sense and awakened only restful thoughts. It was not the vast and sumptuous Père-Lachaise, engulfed and encircled by the houses of the suburbs, enveloped in the perpetual factory smoke of Paris. Here, in the middle of the fields of sainfoins and alfalfa, in the murmuring of the bees and not far from the still waters of a pond above which flew untiring dragonflies, was the smiling melancholy of this country cemetery. The sadness of flowered tombs made one think of a hamlet lost in the distance of solitude, asleep under the sun's heat in the peace of midday.

The recipient of this spiritual connection was like a youth betrothed, experiencing the delicious repose and dialogues interspersed with silences every day of the season, at all hours of the day. Alas, she knew that the silent confidences, the whispered words, the sighs, the sweet plans she experienced were for her inverted hopes, projects of the past. But she did not realize that in the illusion of recreating life, that the life itself was missing and that she was violating death. On the hottest days of September, in the hallucinatory, half-sleep of the heat and the light when she heard only the humming music of flies around her, it seemed several times that her imagination took on a form, and that a light and dark body, seated near her on the mound, spoke to her in a low voice and gently took her hands. With her breathing caught by sudden spasms that came faster in her throat, she listened to the voice that spoke to her with distant inflections, and although it was impossible for her to remember the precise words she had heard, she retained an impression of passionate confidences, long-suppressed complaints which changed into delicious appeasement. Sometimes, too, there was a frenzy of desire to live again, arms of shadow that wanted to hug and knot around her, and a faint mouth that approached her face and searched for her own...

She returned from these meetings and dialogues, sometimes pensive and placid, sometimes nervous and trembling, some days her face burning pink like the roses of the tombs and other days pale, as if she had had met and felt the touch of Death.

The season became rainy, the blue of the mornings and purple of the evening changed into a dull and weeping winter sky. The outings were difficult even in clogs, through the muddy ground of the hostile cemetery. It was necessary to make the visits more infrequent and shorter. Besides, under the cold wind, amidst the dried roses, the dear silhouette did not return, the passionate words were no longer heard.

Her lover seemed to descend deeper into the night, withdrawing each time further into the darkness of the hole where he lay, into the very hollow of the earth towards a more hidden and warm retreat. The vain results of these visits annoyed the persistent visitor and the lover she had found seemed lost again, until she returned to the revitalized candle-lit room and the portrait by the fire, where she continued her investigation.

The bureau was again scrutinized, hidden drawers uncovered, letters similar to the initial ones but continuing them were revealed to the girl. It was then that she finally got to know he who had conquered her through time. An entire beginning of a career, a whole desire for action, was affirmed by this correspondence of ideas, by the manuscripts in which human tenderness pierced through the words of the proud language.

Disappointment seemed to come too: a sealed, knotted notebook, which she opened and began to read, a whole mass of letters in his writing, from the first line she saw they were letters addressed to a woman.

She read quickly at first, with a burning gaze. Passion spoke a beautiful language of desire, eloquently and sadly claiming a share of happiness from the fugitive life. And all this was mixed with stories of dramatic events, a worried love conjoined with the violence of history.

The girl read more closely, pushed further, read false names and quickly convinced herself that she was holding an epistolary novel in the fashion of the time. It was something unique, a novel of unanswered letters, a kind of memoir dedicated to an unknown woman, confidences addressed to the one who does not exist, who will not appear. No doubt a subterfuge, to write all this truth in the form of fiction, to record the regretful love of a man who is a refugee in a ruined city, in a closed house, essaying his social role. A man who knows that he is going to die young.

She gave a cry of tearful joy, looked at the portrait whose pure and luminous eyes also looked at her, and she was convinced that these imaginary letters were addressed to her, that she had finally taken possession of them! That she had come to fetch them where they were because fate had so wished it for him, born too soon, and she, born too late.

And so she was infused, in fever and delusions, with the pain of the irreparable, the feeling of the impossible.

MARIUS & LÉA
(originally published as "Marius & Léa" in *Gil Blas*, April 17, 1893)

THE crime was committed one spring morning, at an hour when the little carriages laden with violets, primroses and lilacs passed by, in one of the "hot streets" of this populous quarter. The terror lasted a long time among the female population who lodged in the flophouses, took their meals in the back shops of the wine merchants, and spent their evenings around the tables of the cafes.

Never had the state of subjection in which the prostitute finds herself vis-a-vis the pimp appeared so clearly as in the phases of this atrocious drama. Truly, there was enough to make melancholy, at least for one evening, the carefree young girls and the experienced veterans who were talking about the event, on the sidewalk and in the shadow of the crossroads, with streams of words and nods of heads. It was not, this time, about an ordinary killing, the periodical news items, the bad encounter with a passing *guest*. That is the usual risk. Such is war.

In this day-to-day life, there is the unexpected of the battlefield, and a creature must reckon with chance. She might look incorrectly at a gentleman, or perhaps she didn't keep her handler close enough to her. The killer leaves, the police are looking for him. And that is the whole story. But in this case things did not happen that way, and everything was terribly precise. This poor Léa was killed by Marius because she refused to feed him, because she did not accept the theft of her jewels.

There had been, at the beginning of the affair, a misunderstanding between the girl and the pimp. The man wanted regularity in his reports. He expected, every morning, to pocket all or part of the previous day's receipts. This was accepted in his world. He knew the fluctuations in the salaries of his comrades, he knew on what sum one could roughly count per month, he foresaw that he would be able to make ends meet and—lo and behold—his calculations already made, his budget established, this Léa refused to enter into the compact and to supply such rigorous accounts.

At first, Marius' astonishment was not very great. He knew this kind of resistance, he knew that it is sometimes necessary to overcome hesitations and tame anger. He therefore resorted to the usual arguments in such cases. He stunned his mistress several times, bruising her with firmly applied punches and kicks. But there was no result, just the continued refusal to communicate the total of the receipt. Marius then contrived to find other ways to reduce this rebellion. He snatched her rings, her earrings, her necklaces, her clothes, and went to sell them. Léa, furious, complained to the district police commissioner.

Marius was wide-eyed in astonishment at this.

He had never seen the police get involved in these sorts of cases. He was indignant and told the tale to others, including some very old rascals who rummaged through their memories, failing to find any trace of a similar event. There was no doubt about it, it was the most serious breach of professional duty on record. In the annals of the profession, transmitted orally during moments of rest or while smoking cigarettes, there was no example of such a refusal of solidarity.

By god, we knew very well that business does not always go as planned, that there are off-seasons and that one cannot, during these periods, be very exacting in relation to the large sum. But everyone then puts their oar in, they manage to get through the difficult times as best as possible. At times when rents are paid, for example, customers become rarer and the pimp must descend into the street, like a wolf out of the woods, and seek additional resources in attacks on the lingering passer-by. He tries to violently take what is not obtained by his partner's persuasion. It's not for his pleasure that he resolves to engage in these brutal tasks as he is generally fat, cowardly, and lazy and he does not seek quarrels except when drunk. But, even so, he needs his two meals, his pints, his game of cards, his tobacco, and he wants to be square with the landlord of the flophouse! He is therefore forced to go out and run at the enemy, after having administered a strong beating to his business partner, who does not know how to guarantee his peace of mind.

So, he goes out, and he balances the budget of his small household.

Marius had never refused this extra work. He was ready to give of himself on the great occasions of unemployment and misery. But it seemed to him that such an acceptance of life together, with its dangers and its possible damage, was well worth a reciprocity of sacrifices and good care, a total confidence of the beloved little woman in the darling little man. And the whole neighborhood, consulted, nodded.

So, his indignation was at its peak when Marius was arrested, taken to the Depot, and sentenced a few days later by the criminal court to four months in prison for theft, assault and battery. Marius' fury increased during these four months. He spent them seeking, inventing, and hatching revenge. When he came out of the cell, in his mind Léa was condemned to death.

Marius met with Léa. He warned her—with a harsh voice, clenched teeth, and the staring eyes of a man determined to kill—of her fate. He settled on the ground floor of the girl's house, in the liquor store where street prostitution has its foundations. A glazed door leads to the back room and its staircase. It is this door which is constantly watched by the pimp, who is prey to the fixed idea, the frightful amorous spite of a lover who has been refused his tobacco, his little glasses, his slippers and his pocket money! Twice, he opened this door, climbed the first steps of the staircase. Those two times, the concierge prevented him from going upstairs, holding him at bay with a revolver.

One morning his guard is deceived, and for a third time the agile Marius climbs the steps four by four. His Léa, his former mistress, will not escape him this time. He heads after her with impulsive instincts, with the muscular decision of a wild beast sure of its prey. He rings the bell. The girl half-opens the door.

The door is forced by his shoulder, the bed is thrown against the door with another push. A kitchen knife in hand, the frightening man falls on the woman with wide eyes and an open, mute mouth. He seized her by the hair, threw her to the ground, and cut off her head with a sudden stroke.

A neighbor, who does not dare enter on threat of being shot with a revolver, went to look for the police. But it's all over. During all this coming and going, Marius has finished killing and takes the severed head, tying it by the hair to the handle of the window shutter. Showing it to passers-by, he called the crowd under the window, sneering as he performed an awful spiel of love and revenge. Then, when the door is finally forced open, he blew his brains out.

It is this frightful adventure that it is spoken of in the nocturnal meetings and in the intimacy of the households of prostitution, in this corner of the suburb.

The memory of the butchery from this sector comes back like a threat through reproaches, it shows in the tears, giving rise to fear and presentiment in the fatalistic soul of the girls, it passes quickly in the troubled looks exchanged during those base discussions amid heavy drunkenness. And almost all give their approval and admiration to the killer. Marius is applauded like a criminal who died on the gallows. He didn't hide, he didn't run, he didn't try to fight a jury for his life. He only wanted people to know that he was killing and why he was killing. He punished, in cold blood, a lack of explanation and a breach of contract.

Léa, for her part, is insulted for having had her lover arrested, and even for having caused his death. This is how gossip creates legends.

None of the sad larvae wandering at these crossroads think, raising their eyes towards the crime chamber, of anything but that tense and pale head, disgusting and bloody, which was one day hung there, above the house number, a symbolic sign for a dreadful and martyring profession.

THE VOICE
(originally published as "La voix" in *Le Cœur Et L'esprit*, 1894)

AT that time I lived in a six-story house, which was served by one of those twisted and vertiginous staircases suggesting the bourgeois bitterness of the owners. The architect who had arranged the narrow steps and swinging ramp by which one climbed this dream vision, undoubtedly understood the requirements of cost and profit which are the determining considerations in this commercial district's industry and trade. Not a square or cubic centimeter of space had been lost. The necessary (but *only* the necessary) space was conceded to the occupants of stores and houses jumbled as far as the eye could see, from the ground to the clouds. The corridors, used only as landings, offered to the confused observer an extraordinary multiplicity of doors covered with labels, names, and signs of all kinds. The tiny windows, harmonized with the style of the building, let in enough light to grope and prevented the need of gaslight in daytime. The scientifically designed air intakes provided just enough oxygen supply essential for breathing. Finally, the width of the staircase, strictly measured, allowed the difficult movement of dismantled and infinitely fragmented furniture with the simultaneous passage of two poorly fed, very thin people meeting in random ascensions and tumbling descents.

Between these close walls, in these spirals and conditions of cramp and chiaroscuro with their inevitable rustlings and shocks, it became almost impossible to ignore the people who were met at the corner of this narrow maze. However, with the thoughtful concentration and social solitude I dwelt, I paid little attention to those who indifferently touched the outer circle of my existence. Leaving in the morning to tramp the city or wander the fields, I did not return to my sixth floor to work until the evening, when the doors and shutters were closed and I was insensitive to the sounds of the human menagerie in whose midst I had set up a sufficient spot. When descending, my concerns were light, and when returning, I was heavy with thoughts from outside, so I passed through the improbably constricting cage of this staircase like an empty bucket slowly drawn up, filled, between the long cylindrical walls of a well. I was very young, by the way, little concerned about tangible realities, and it would not have occurred to me that I had only to look around at the beings and things immediately surrounding me to find the intimacies and generalizations, the depths of sensations and strangeness of existence in all of them which feeds the avid observer.

So I passed without seeing the near-elegance of the first floors and the badly aged liveries of the further heights. I did not in any way fix my interest on the incessant comings and goings of the clerks, the sorrowful men, the seamstresses, the architectural engineers and the good maids. Then, one day, my attention was abruptly caught by a silhouette that crossed the field of my vision. I descended, and for a moment I kept hearing the step of a climber, a slow, steady, supported, mechanical pace. When the being I heard below moved into the dim light I drew myself back, as I usually did when people laden with burdens passed. It was a woman who moved near me, and she certainly focused my usually distracted eyes. I had never before passed this insignificant apparition. Almost a dwarf, badly constructed, short-legged, her long arms hung straight against her body. She looked like a being escaped from a German tale, one of those pencil fantasies where the limbs and the trunk disagree, a chance welding made in a hospital of clippings from humanity. The whole thing made one think of a gross sliding, a rough interlocking, a bad mechanism. Legs tucked into the body, hands dangling, sometimes randomly waving to feel the ramp or the wall, this unsuccessful construct of a woman walked with a stiffness, a large and awkward rhythm that shook her whole frame. She paraded in front of me like an automaton of wood, without seeming to suspect my presence, without replying to the few words of excuse that I murmured when leaning against the wall of the corridor. She quickly disappeared, but that short span was all that was necessary for her form to be engraved in my memory. Above this body, as it came, I had furtively seen only her straightly held head, with a fixed, blind eye and a vaguely angular and ruddy face. I stood for a moment listening to the footsteps that echoed and were lost in the dark, spiraling staircase, drawn upwards as if into the steeple of a cathedral.

Obviously, I had not yet been introduced to this mechanical, shuffling sleepwalker. Had she moved in recently, and had I just not paid any attention to the moving men's cries and bangs of knocked furniture? Did she live parallel to me, going out and returning at other times than mine? Or was she just a passing worker, or a visitor, coming at rare intervals, who I might never see again? But then, she carried no bundle and the poor people who work all day hardly receive visitors. So, rather, I thought her likely to be a new tenant. But in spite of my awakening curiosity, I asked no questions and manifested nothing of the violent intellectual desire for espionage to which I was prey. I had never had a useful conversation with the building superintendent, and I hardly exchanged with my neighbors—all sedentary manufacturers constantly at their work—more than the mundane "good day" and "good evening," or observations on the rain and weather.

I did not resolve myself and yet, without an act of will on my part, I managed to gain information. Over the next few days, returning to my room for the midday meal, I again met the woman in the hallway, on the stairs, and even in the surrounding streets. She usually carried a milk box, a bowl of broth, or a jar of lentils in which a piece of boiled meat was dipped, and soon I suspected her of devout practices. On some evenings of that sweet spring, through the dimly tinted shades of gold and violet that lurk at sunset, I saw a recognizable figure shuffling along the gray wall of the nearby church and convent, disappearing through the door of a side-alley or speaking through the grille of a peephole. Moreover, one morning I saw her going up the avenue with an armful of branches to bless, and I began to become fixated on the question of her occupation.

A widow or old maid, no doubt, prayerful, earning a few *sous* from her livelihood as a dispenser of holy water, dusting chairs, burning candles. Her face, especially on that Palm Sunday, seen in full light, proved irretrievably ugly, not the ordinary ugliness that arises from a derangement of the appearance or the indulgence of ill will, but instead the ugliness of a will eager to kill expression, eager to complicate a human face with the bestial. A low forehead sprouted discolored red hair, cheekbones, a jaw, a bony chin and, above all, the faint illumination of two white eyes covered with a glaze, almost empty of sight. Her approach, always the same, was of heavy and slow steps, a jerky and resounding pace.

✳

I no longer thought of the unfortunate woman—giving her the same attention as a fairy-tale character, that is to say a little disgust mingled with pity—when an inexplicable fact brutally disturbed my indifference, collecting my scattered sensitivity and disturbing the depths of my dormant existence.

One evening I was reading in my room by the last falling daylight, scarcely distracted by the cries of returning swallows, when the confused sound of conversation came to murmur in my ear. I did not immediately seek where the muttering was coming from, as this house was usually noisy with singing, shouting, hammering, and squeaking machines. But my ears could not help but feel a softness coming from these indistinct, whispered words. Then the sensation increased. A strangely musical resonance passed through the wall, then another, then again, reminiscent of the sounds of instruments tuned at the beginning of a concert, prelude of future harmonies. And yet it was, no doubt, human words that I heard.

Moved, sensitive as I am to the differences of accents and the timbres of voices, I got up and went to the frail slatted and plastered partition that served as a wall, and stuck my ear to it. I felt a wonderful pleasure I had never experienced before. I listened closely, with an inner frenzy that made my heart beat tumultuously. Yes, it was a concert I was hearing, a most unexpected concert! An extraordinary voice filled my neighbor's narrow studio, a deep, domineering voice that sounded like echoes in a marble palace, rising and beating the air like the wild song of a nightingale in an evening park, languishing and dying like the endless sentence of a cello. I exhaust the most dissimilar comparisons in wanting to describe that voice which was far superior to an orchestra, that surprising double voice which passed from the viola to the mezzo-soprano without discernible connections, which summed up in turn or almost at once *all* of the instruments, the deep, the vibrating, the subtle, and added to it the living charm of a delicious sound passing through a human mouth! I squeezed against the wall as if I wanted to embed myself in it. The thin masonry filtered the sounds which darted into the most acute parts of my brain and went through me like a river of waves. I could not regain possession of myself until the voice was silent. Then, in my mind and my senses, there was a moment's pause during which, as I rested, I perceived nothing of the vulgar dialogue that commenced. The voice would then resume, and with it my passionate attention. I did not understand what was being said, despite the brilliant sound of those uncanny words, and I was only affected by that deep song that my ears had never before heard. The words that came to me seemed to stand out like melodic reminders of a symphony's weave. At last the conversation fell away, there was a sound of moving chairs and simultaneously a laugh unlike anything I could have ever imagined, a laugh scattered like a rain of gold coins, tinkling in the manner of a prodigious harmonica, rising, spreading, a finale to this incomprehensible opera from a single voice, played in the poor staging of this sixth floor.

Footsteps went to the door. I threw myself out of my room, determined to hear again, and finally see the source of the voice. I arrived just in time to find, exiting my neighbors' quarters, a maid in a white apron, a rather pretty girl, along with the woman from the staircase. They were silent when they saw me, and turned down the darkened corner of the corridor. I followed them, turned down the corridor, which

I had never before traversed, but saw no one, no moving shadow in the dark. I heard footsteps creaking on the badly joined deal boards, however, stepped forward and soon stumbled into an almost vertical ladder, barely visible in the evening grayness falling from dusty granaries. So, unbeknownst to me, the house had a seventh floor and the two women had gone up, disappearing into that fading sunlight without a word. I retreated, perplexed, angry, watching for the slightest disruption in the restored silence. Soon, a single step came down again, moved closer. I showed myself, determined to know everything and relieve my suffering from incertitude. It was the fair maid in the white apron who emerged from the shadows. Surely, I thought, this robust brunette had that music in her voice and laughter. I asked her an idle question about the time, I think. She blushed, smiled, passed a wavering look as perhaps she thought this was the beginning of pursuit, and answered in a voice accented by the central provinces. So, I was wrong. But then…? What thoughts crossed my mind! I rushed almost madly to my neighbor's, not conscious of my actions, determined at following every action, improper or not, to find out who owned that voice that still resounded in my head. My neighbors, a couple, were alone, and I knew both of them possessed sluggish, Parisian voices. There was no more hesitation possible. The one that had penetrated me with an irresistible charm, who had enveloped me in an atmosphere impossible to dispel, was the singular, groping, sexless and ugly person from the corridor.

The extent of my misfortune seemed un-limited, for the evoked vision of that dwarf could not dissolve the impression of delight which possessed me entirely. I began a hasty conversation with the couple, random and unrelated, which might have revealed my incomprehensible confusion if my neighbors had been more perspicacious, but they no-ticed nothing. The man continued shaping an object held by a vise while the woman, while tending the room, answered all my demand-ing questions about the house and its tenants, in an almost curt voice. She described to me, in her talkative spiel, all the house's inhabi-tants, present and past, and I had to let her unfold the history of this Parisian place until she had arrived at the seventh floor, whose skylight windows opened like hatches to the sky. I put on a show of interest, which excited her commentary, and soon learned from this boring tour part of what was worrying my thoughts so cruelly.

The attic above the low, paneled rooms of the sixth floor, that garret (whose existence I had been unaware of) was inhabited by a colony of aged widows, neglected, sedentary invalids fed on government vouchers. There were pale, slender women in black bonnets, retired servants living on pensions of fifteen francs a month made by charitable masters, nourishing their diminished carcasses for three days with beef stew costing twelve *sous*. The one that haunted my thoughts wouldn't fit any specific category. They knew she did nothing, they did not know if she had ever done anything. They did not know her age. Maybe she was fifty, maybe she was only twenty-five. Her sight was feeble and forbade her to work, but perhaps there was some feint there, for she walked up and down the stairs with straightness and surprising assurance, slowly moving her short and massive legs, prudently placing her feet one in front of the other. A perpetual beggar, accustomed to churches, she never returned without booty, obtained frequent double rations, and was the recipient of exceptional care. The watchmaker of the convent came every two weeks to set her clock, the hairdresser—who had devout clientele—combed and arranged her hair, powdering her face with a hint of rice flower, and the benevolent ladies gave her rags from their tired toilets. She ate like an ogress, and dressed like a coquette. She wore old, patched silk stockings and button-down boots, her petticoat and camisole were passable, and she wore on her head, instead of a cap, a hat with a veil draped down the back, which gave her the look of a poor London gin-drunk. Additionally, as soon as a man spoke to her, she acted troubled and mimed like she were beside herself.

Of her voice, there was no mention, and so on this subject I remained craftily reserved, being careful not to risk the slightest allusion, seeming to interest myself only in the cunning of this poor woman. I was sure that my neighbors had not noticed anything about that extra-human voice that had stirred the depths of my being. They even observed, with a certain irony, that for a few days the woman had dressed up and chosen a place in the chapel, against a pillar, and left every evening to sing with the girls for May: the month of Mary.

I withdrew with the most indifferent air I could put on my nervous discomfort. Back home, I tried to coldly judge the state I was in, but I could not do it. I wished to satisfy my imperious desire and obey the impulse that carried my will. The following days I used to seek the means of attracting to my abode, to possessing for myself alone, to enjoy until satiety, that incomprehensible Voice which followed me everywhere, which broke forth in the restless sleep of my nights. I was in unknown territory and did not know what, if any, pretext would work for me to capture this strange, perhaps ominous individual whom I knew only by her character and habits but whose substance I had no knowledge of. Regardless, I promised myself to act on our next meeting.

Indeed, I did act. One evening, when the woman was passing by my door, I proposed that she enter and take what might be convenient for her from among the utensils and useless clothes that my family had left me. She entered without saying a word, her step heavy, and walked all over, snooping like a beast. I gave her my rubbish sparingly, wanting to attract her again. She had a blush in her cheeks, her movements were febrile, and although I avoided weighing my inquisitive eyes upon her, I only snatched a few monosyllables from her. But those monosyllables, stated clearly as if by a trumpet of precious metal, entered my heart and made me reel.

We continued like that for a few days, she not giving more of herself, not speaking more than she needed to, but choosing to return. My provision of faded ribbons and tired velvet were beginning to run out when, with an abrupt and enchanting word, she offered to give my household some obligatory care and mend my best linens in exchange for my presents, despite the tiredness of her eyes. The room where I lived and its poverty were sufficient to allow me to accept this offer of service from a woman living on charity. And since then, at a time I had chosen, she came to my house to touch my things with her heavy hands.

I had chosen the evening hours for these visits, that soothing dusk when the sun goes down and continues into the semi-darkness when lamps are lit. I could not bring my-self to see, with full clarity, her ugliness and vulgarity. Her face pushed my eyes away as they ventured to fix on it. The distant ears, the brutal nose, the brutish skull, were one of the saddest deformations of a human face that could ever be seen. The colorless eyes, as gloomy as stagnant ponds, filled one with a sort of vertigo when contemplated. The mouth itself, which should have been shaped for the sounds it emitted, was instead soft and shapeless, opening on irregular teeth. When I looked at this woman, who always wore a hat like some crazy Salpêtrière resident, my heart beat and I was invaded by a disgust impossible to quell. Those first days, I endured her presence with difficulty. But when she began to speak, I forgot everything. And soon, used to my ways and taken by the sweetness of my room as it glowed with the fires of the sunset, she showed herself as an inexhaustible talker and, soon, began speaking the moment she entered, only ceasing as she exited into the corridor. And I followed her there, as if led on a leash by the golden chains of her voice.

But what was this supernatural voice? What form produced it? What strings of metal stretched in that throat? From what crystal, what unknown diamond in her mysterious larynx generated such sounds, whence came the celestial glottis that emitted them?

And how could this song not expire in contact with these cheeks and that mouth?

How did it vibrate with this force, carried by her breath? It was necessary to give up on explaining it. As I appeared occupied with reading or writing, I dared not raise my eyes to her and limited myself to reviving the conversation when it threatened to fall. Such incidents were rare. As she worked on a worn handkerchief or shirt, she talked, talked, talked indefatigably.

I listened. That voice, harmonious and varied, had conquered me. Sometimes as light as a breeze, with sweet couplings like sighs, more often authoritarian, imperious, full like an organ, grave, elevated and pathetic, precipitating like the language of a passionate soul. At times there followed lively variations, the changing finesses of a clear hymn that would rise ever higher in a subtle air, then the sharp and deep articulations of a unified chorus resounding in a crypt. Buried in the darkest corner of my room, I never tired of listening to those waves of harmony, nestling as this ragged seamstress painfully sewed in the last glow of dusk that was dying at the window.

Even today, long after it all, I cannot remember what banal words ran in the modulation of her voice. Did I know it even then, during the moments of this awful and delicious spring? Had I really only paid small attention to the meaning of this gossip so beautifully and unconsciously orchestrated?

It seems to me now, looking back, that the words were not absolutely devoid of interest and that the sad creature had the proud, fierce, and slightly exalted character exhibited by many miserable prisoners of life, having long pondered fixed thoughts that were pointed at maniacally. In her gait she reminded me a little of hikers I had seen, wandering in the plains strewn with raised stones which surround the hamlets of Brittany, between Plouescat and Lesneven, melancholically singing. It was evidently there, in those grayish plains dotted with goldenrod and mourning-veiled by the violet heather bloom, that she ought to have lived her despised existence, keeping goats and gathering wool. She should have spoken her soliloquies and melancholy laments, her voice swelling like the surf, among the pebbles on shores of desolate seas, surprising and stupefying travelers immobilized at a path's turning. But then, what did I care about what could have been? I did not inquire of the country where the woman was born, I knew nothing of her previous life, did not learn her age, did not even ask her name. In the grip of a veritable obsession, I waited all day for her to come and, when the hour of our strange rendezvous arrived, it was enough for me just to be there and speak. I released myself to all the melodic phrases that fluttered past, whirling through my room to shatter on the low ceiling or fly through the open window into the bloody sky of the day's ending. I fell into hollow, abyssal dreams from which analysis was absent. I resorted to childishness to exalt my feeling, giving myself a musical theme of Beethoven, Chopin, or Wagner to develop into a sentence relative to the disposition of where I was and the particular sound of my punctual visitor's voice. I ended up going to church, in the evening hours, where the white and blue sisterhood sang in front of the altar of the Virgin, bathed with light. And even there I was plagued by excessive raptures. I could distinguish the Voice, the only voice that answered my anxious thoughts, through all the choruses and all the accompaniments. That voice alone filled the church, wrapped itself around the pillars, vibrated in the windows, rang through the vaults. She would go through the deepest registers and descend into those cellars of music where the notes of the tenth-century songs are so skillfully spaced, or dance on the highest, most aerial peaks with the cries of the wounded turtledove. It was she whom I heard, she who was, by a kind of bizarre transposition, visible to the eyes of my mind.

It was on returning, enervated, from one of those evenings that with a shameful terror I understood the true character of the sickly anxiety that possessed me. I felt myself pierced by an indefinable jealousy that mingled the present and the future of my life. I had the conviction that this voice that was discovered by me, also belonged to me, and I felt a rage to see it lavished on others, not just given to the indifferent assistance of nocturnal services in offering to this insensitive religion. I envisioned my future self, freed from daily trouble, exposing a few rare individuals or, yes, keeping selfishly, this joyful sound. In a cleverly arranged environment, behind a shaking curtain, this unique voice would proclaim the verses and prose of some poet, the melodies of some musician. And I had the clear and sudden conviction that the chapel might rob me of most of my future happiness.

That's when the truth came to me.

My worry was the concern of a lover. My presentiments, my arrangements for the future, were proofs of an indissoluble attachment which bound my being to this voice.

My sweat froze then, as if I had seen myself reflected. I got scared, and yet I silenced my reason, which stammered some small objections. No, I did not want to stop seeing her physical degradation, her lowered condition. Certainly, there were more beautiful, more elegant lovers. But which of them could have equaled what this despised one possessed, alone among all the women? Yes, I confessed to myself with a raging pride, yes, I loved her for her voice! Why not? Others fall for eyes of blue or black, long hair, a row of white teeth, or arms, legs, breasts or sex, for the wits, for kindness. But show them and let them admit that all else wanting, that ugliness dwells permanently on the face they kiss and adore.

Perhaps they will admit it, but they will also celebrate the quality that conquered them, the charm that embalmed them alive, that fixed and mummified their lives at the feet of the idol. They have found, like alchemists, the crucible where love is constantly reborn, and all that other men seek is nothing to them. And I was so. I, too, had found it and I wanted to stick to my discovery. I was enslaved by that voice, distance from which made me desperate and feverish. I still felt that I needed it, and forever would. Doubtless, I did not find in this passion the outcome ordinarily sought: the idea of possessing this woman caused me real horror. But then the carnal communion, as it currently existed between us, seemed to me sufficiently agitating and voluptuous.

The next day, when the one who enchanted me came to my door to sit, I tried to mate our voices in discussion, as a result of the reflections that had long oppressed me during the painful insomnia of the preceding night. With my shy, thin speech I tried to penetrate the astonishing splendor of this organ that evoked flesh, marble, and metal. But no, the union was impossible, and it was necessary to leave the double voice to her duets of head and heart, to her alternating phrases cut by breaths resembling the final sighs of a woman in love. Our union was half material, half spiritual, and that link was established—who could say through what unknown ways— from her words of flame to my feverish brain.

I lived the whole month of May not knowing what to do, going from hope to discouragement, living in the exalted world of nightmares or sleeping in the heavy calm of prostration.

Now I do not doubt that it was this irresolution which brought about the end of that liaison which filled my days. And this thought will always poison my life.

One evening, she who I hoped for did not come. I waited an hour, two hours, opening my door, listening for noises, like a lover suffering from the delay of his mistress. Nothing. I ventured stealthily along the wobbly and creaking stairs of the seventh floor. I crawled through a maze of low capped corridors. A door was opened. The day ended on the horizon and the rising moon illuminated her room, empty. Not a piece of furniture, just the four walls. I did not have a moment of doubt. She had lived in this loft and she had left. I went down again. My neighbor showed her curious head, watching my comings and goings. What did I care! I stopped on her landing, listening to the woman's story, with its interlaced words and that happy shudder peculiar to the talkative. Yes, the one I was asking after had left the house during the day. The move was neither long nor complicated.

Her furniture and her gear had all been held in one carriage, they could have been removed by the hook of the commissionaire! Where did she go? To the nuns in the convent, locked in, cloistered. Yes, permanently and forever. No one returned from that house of reclusion. On the recommendation of a confessor, who took pity on the poor, they were going to make her a kind of Beguine, a half-nun in apron and white cap. She would have a cell, take care of a few quiet tasks during the day, and never go out again. The courtyards and gardens were enough for walks. Ah, and do you understand that these ladies, who never cross the threshold of their convent, who receive no one, who do not even let them in for their mass, said that the newcomer would sing at the offices in the organ gallery, every morning, every evening, at every ceremony, to Darkness during Holy Week, at Mass, at Vespers, Compline, Sunday Greetings, at the Matins of each night?

Did I understand? My jealousy of those May evenings were justified. The church, for which the charmed one sang, had heard her joyful sound. And now the silent, locked, dead house delighted in this abject and bewitching creature! They had abducted her, took her from me without any warning or farewell between us! They imprisoned her and raised a wall between us! What days, what evenings, I spent prowling around that silent house! Even now, after resignation has engulfed me like the tumult of high tide, even now at certain hours, especially during the intermediate duration of dusk, it awakens in me terrible regrets, furious desires, and I run. I run up to those walls, to those bars, wanting one last time to hear the Voice! The Voice for which I am nostalgic, the voice which made me insensitive to any joy of the eyes and even—O abomination!—to all the satisfaction of intelligence, that Voice which, on leaving, has filled my mind and heart with loneliness.

THE POSSESSED

(Originally published as "La Possédée" in
La Lanterne, August 3, 1895)

THE windmill turns in the middle of
fields and moors. Its ragged wings, which
make one think of great flocks of birds and
the swelling of the sails of a boat, rise, oscillate
and fall, slowly, then quickly. The moving
shadows pass over the ground like shivers. The
mill turns sadly under the December sky.

There is winter in the air, cold, rain, maybe
snow. The earth is in mourning for all greenery and all flowers. There are only a few shrubs
of a dark color, bristling with thorns, furze,
and brambles. The dazzling yellow flowers
of the gorse, the pink bunches of heather are
rust-colored and soiled by the muddy water,
ruffled by the wind blowing from the sea. The
rutted ground is dotted with marshy puddles,
cluttered with stones. The hedges, all black,

are empty of birds. Here and there stand the solitary raised stones, gnawed by parasitic moss, the coarse menhirs which make one think of the harshness and bloodshed of ancient beliefs. The mill grinder still spins with a slight hiss and creak. As we approached, we would hear the scraping of millstones and the crushing of grain.

So there is life behind those walls, under those pointed roofs, in this round tower which resounds with the songs of the miller. All the people of this village grouped nearby, around these bare trees which will be green again soon, bring a share of the wheat from their harvest. They have attached their beast, horse or donkey, to this rusty ring. They enter through this door, they chat with the flour-maker, heavy footsteps make the ladder creak, bags fall surrounded by a fine white cloud. There is, no doubt, a coming and going of the living around this hovel, the landscape is not always so desolate and so sad, there comes a season when the warblers go to sing under the useless menhirs.

The village is in the Morbihan region of Brittany. The mill is the Jallu mill. The miller is mother Jallu, she has four children, two sons and two daughters.

The sons and one of the daughters never sing, perhaps. They are peasants with worried foreheads, melancholy eyes, who walk heavily and watch from aside. But never a finer miller than Esther Jallu has turned and turned around wheat, buckwheat, barley, rye and oats. The little girl is cheerful because she is pretty and knows how to wear the dresses she has made and hemmed herself. Like a fairy she crosses the sad autumn countryside, so sweet in spring. In her unconsciousness, as a child and a woman, she imagines herself a sort of comic opera miller in this harsh Breton country of rocky earth and rough foliage. For a time she might put bunches of ribbons on her clogs, or cut her bodice into a square or a heart. The light dust of the ground flour in the hutches powders her hair, which has escaped the embroidery of her headdress.

She went to school longer and with more enthusiasm than her brothers and sister, and she retained what she was taught on the blackboard and in books. In the evening with her family, gathered around the table where the soup steams, she speaks guttural Breton, through which passes the sounds of wind, waves and pebbles. But she also knows, better than anyone in the countryside, how to speak French, set up an account, write a letter. She will be an orderly housewife, a smart woman, she will bring happiness to whoever marries her.

The suitors are not lacking, moreover, but she is careful not to decide. She is waiting. Why? It's the secret of this brave girl's heart which beats under the well-ironed wimple. When the day comes, she will know how to choose. Until then, she keeps her own thoughts, she responds with a phrase of mockery or with a laugh of contentment to her astonished family who does not understand and constantly obsesses over her with their suspicious glances.

So, she continues to live carefree, prettier every day, walking her proud maturity in the middle of the assemblies where the suitors come to surround her, in the wedding meals where they sing songs for her which offer engagement and invitations to wed. She constantly adorns herself, looking for the prettiest handkerchiefs, the finest shoes. She consoles herself from the bad moods that rise around her and assail her by adding a flower to the bouquet that perfumes her bosom.

Irritation and anger fill the house, an irritation that growls dully, an anger that barely speaks through gritted teeth. There are hands that withdraw and bodies that fade as Esther approaches. The young girl sees, when she enters, a fear rising in the eyes of her mother and her sister, she sees a mad fury ignite in the eyes of her brothers. She is watched like a sick person, kept at a distance like a plague victim. She shrugs and passes. The two men and the two women look at each other, tap their foreheads knowingly, approach each other, consult in low voices.

They now know what situation their daughter and their sister is in, they know the reason for her pride, her joy, her laughter and her songs, they know what enemy is hounding her, they know the name of the Evil that has struck her. This name, the rector has told them. They met the fellow in the fields, they accompanied him to his presbytery, they told him of their fears, their grief, and the fellow spoke. Stopping in the middle of the path, and closing his breviary, he informed them, with a moaning voice, that Esther is possessed by the demon of pride! Then the priest returned home. He was not a good adviser, the wise man who warns and explains, but poor in spirit, the worst of all, the pretentious phrase-maker.

There is no more doubt. The explanation is given. Possessed! She is possessed! Inhabited by a demon! There is no longer any wonder why all the men run after the flirt, and if she has bewitched them, bewitched in her turn the old people who walk leaning on their sticks, the young people who drive the plow, the women who knit on the doorstep, the children who play in the squares. Because she has cast a spell on everyone, everyone loves her and comes to her, and smiles at her, and cries for her spells. Whereas they, the brothers, the sister, she—the old woman, the mother, they are hated, sometimes insulted, and little girls run away when they see them appear. But that must change. They have to spread the word of the priest, tell everyone that a demon lives in Esther's body, and that the four of them, the Jallu family, will know how to exorcise the unfortunate woman and extirpate the beast from hell that is eating away at her brain and heart.

That's why one day, while the mill turns under the December sky, the door was locked from the inside. All you could hear is the creaking of the gears, the hissing of the blades, the scraping of the millstones. The wind passes and the rain falls. Inside, gnarled hands, clenched and hard as oak roots, seized her by the arm, the thigh, the waist, this white-powdered, delicate miller girl. The two men threw her on the ground, they lifted her skirts, exposed her young girl's flesh, and now, with a crankshaft, they pierce her belly, they turn and turn the instrument. The blood flows, the mouth screams and cries. A hole is also made in one leg, then in the other, a hole in the forehead, and blood flows, again and again. Mother and sister are on their knees. They pray for the operation to succeed. It succeeds, the demon flees. Esther doesn't move. The exorcists get up, slide and flounder, exchange looks of madness. The mill is still turning, but the miller is dead.

THE TRUE FEAR
(originally published as "La Vraie Peur" in *La Lanterne*, October 12, 1895)

THE young woman was informed about the whole of existence, the instincts of nature and its ferocities and social perversities, by a banal incident of everyday life. She seldom left her lover, had gotten into the habit of accompanying him almost anywhere the necessities of his profession and the hassles of business formalities called him. When the boredom might be too prolonged or she would have just been standing around, she stayed at home. He willingly, as well, agreed to follow her wherever she was called by the demands of the household, or by her womanly whims of utility or pleasure: to a supplier, in the maze of a department store, in some theater, exhibition, closed party or out in the open air.

He was never bored with this perpetual camaraderie. He knew that, regardless of the interlocutor, one has little more than dialogues with oneself, that conversation affirms a community of tastes or manifests a violence of contrasts and a tearing of antipathies. The presence of this charming girl was therefore always a delight to him. Everything she said, in her vivid and unreflective visions of things, was to him a good pretext to more closely examine and understand the most assertive thoughts and solidly substantiated dissertations from books.

The great raw material that feeds all dreams also gives birth to all experience, as it is life. And life appears at all times in all beings, makes a glimmer of its mystery shine through all eyes, gives an echo of its secret to all voices. There are no questions more far reaching and more precisely stated than the questions of a child.

The woman who passes herein in silhouette had the soul of a child. She walked through the streets, traversed the multitudes and left them in the wake of her skirts, in exactly the same state of mind in which she found herself at the theatre. Things appeared to her like a succession of stage sets and humanity like an immense figuration. She saw only very vaguely these appearances, moreover. Attached to her lover's arm, she gazed without seeing, bursting into exaltation of words, and only stopped talking to watch her companion speak.

※

One autumn day after a walk together, they had separated to meet again later, towards the end of the afternoon. They had made an appointment in the great alley—usually frequented by an elegant, amiable-looking crowd—of one of those beautiful gardens in Paris where the trees, the pools with their man-made fountains, the statuary of lower gods, and the lawns were all lit up with flowers to create the enchantment of a park in the middle of the tall buildings of the city.

She was there on time, and quite surprised—not that she had appeared first, but that the meeting did not take place at the exact minute. She waited, he did not come, and here is the story that she told him of her waiting when they found themselves in their home:

"Oh! my dear Lucien, I'm not angry with you, and I understand now that it was impossible for you to join me, but what adventures! I wasn't bored at first. It was still a little warm, and I sat down, not thinking too much about anything. I watched the clouds passing very slowly. I was looking at the flowers that were motionless, and it seemed to me that they were looking at me too. Then, I got a little cold, I left my seat, and I walked slowly all along the pathway. That's when I started to feel worried. I feared for you, but I didn't know why I was scared.

"The evening had come, the sky that was so red earlier at sunset was gradually becoming purple. The large flowers which had seemed motionless to me swayed like ghosts. I could no longer see their colors, all had become pale.

"It was then that I realized that I was not alone in the garden. A moment before, I wasn't paying attention to the people walking by, and suddenly I saw myself surrounded by shadows. They wandered around me, constantly coming closer, slipping around the trees, hiding behind the clumps. How I would have liked to see you appear! I wanted to go away, and I didn't dare, so I tried to put on a good face under all those eyes watching me.

"Through the branches I saw a light flare. At first I thought it was moonlight, but it was an electric light, very far away, and I found the darkness even darker around me. Night had now come. I had to leave, I no longer knew my way, I was terrified by all these shadows watching me. I walked, I threw myself down a back alley. I then saw that I was followed by two shadows, and having completely lost my head, instead of going out into the street, I found myself on the quay.

"I left the wall for the middle of the road. The shadows had joined me, I saw them, I heard them. They passed and repassed around me, in front of me, behind me. Two thugs, two horrible figures. One complained, the other sneered. One showed me his wrapped hand, spoke to me of a wound… of a hospital…. of bread. The other was swearing at me with words I didn't understand. Both were threatening, both frightened me. I thought they were going to hit me, my legs were shaking, I was covered in a cold sweat, and I couldn't find a word to cry out.

"I thought of everything I had read in the newspapers, of the women cut to pieces, of the assassins being guillotined, of those who have disappeared. I, who read the news items as I read the serial novel, without really knowing what happened for real, I now thought I was walking between two famous assassins. Without daring to turn my head, without daring to open my eyes, I saw the gestures to my right and to my left, a hand wrapped in rags that wanted to take my sleeve, a clenched fist that approached ever closer to my face.

"A cab passed, I approached it, and the two silhouettes disappeared. Another appeared, a well-dressed man, wrapped in a fur coat, and he invited me with greetings to enter the cab. He spoke in a somewhat low voice, but I could see his eyes and his teeth shining, and he frightened me even more than the others. And, on the other side of the cab, there appeared another, similar man, obsequious, engaging, who also opened the door. Regardless, I didn't know what I was seeing anymore. I panicked, trembling, and I ran away pursued by cries and laughter. I arrived at the lights, at the omnibus office, stared at by everyone. Men appeared to me with hard eyes and voracious jaws. They seemed to hold back from throwing themselves at me. The women looked contemptuous. As I approached, I heard someone talking to me again, someone in front of me, leaning over, saying, 'I'm a decent man,' though he looked like a brute. I was dying of shame, I felt flushed and hot, I stumbled down to my door. Oh, my darling, if I had to live without you, if I found myself alone in all this world, what would become of me?..."

She was tearful and quivering. He took her hands and answered her:

"My dear Denise, you have known real fear, the only real one, the only one that can be proven. What imagined fear could be compared to that one, which is felt in contact with one's fellow human in a full, civilized environment? All the rest is a fantasy conception, a chimera born of our fever. In haunted houses, in old castles full of the sound of chains, where the cold air moves as ghosts pass, all these appearances vanish in the morning. In the countryside, at night, it is we who interpret shapes and noises in the direction of our fears, it is we who people the solitude with all the ghosts we carry within us. Admittedly, this fear exists, and some cannot defend themselves from it. But it is very conventional and easily defeated compared to the sudden sensation and crushing revelation, you had.

"You had the fear of instinct, and not only because you were the woman chased by the man, but also because you were the weak met by the strong. All animal species live continuously in the anxiety that you have known for a random half-hour. The ocean is replete with furtive escapes and greedy pursuits. The forest is constantly traversed by the fear of deer and the hunger of wolves. In the spaces of the air, the hawk always seeks the lark.

"And the big city conceals enslavement and carnage, like the air, the forest and the ocean. You read *Robinson Crusoe* when you were a little girl. And now you understand the admirable moment of that solitary man's first fright. He feared neither the land nor the sea, nor the noise he heard at night around his cabin. But all his blood rushed and froze around his heart, and he turned white as a corpse when he saw, on the cool sand of the beach—the clear, irrefutable, frightening imprint of the foot of a man."

THE SCULPTOR'S WIFE
(originally published as "La Femme du Sculpteur" in *La Lanterne*, February 13, 1896)

DURING the days of engagement, contract and the wedding, when the young girl chose, accepted and then married the young sculptor, she understood more or less what to expect about the special existence that she was definitely going to have and practice. She had lived, from her beginnings as a young socialite, in a region of brilliant luxury, feverish distractions, and fashionable literature where the "actors" in Parisian life parade. In the prying chatter and angry conversation that make up the atmosphere of such an environment, if everything is not said at least everything is insinuated. There are young girls who don't understand—and others who understand. Some pass through these most scandalous years, these most informative commentaries, without losing any of their flowery down, their virginal candor, their childlike naivete. Some also know right away what it is and find themselves possessing, without anyone knowing how it can be done and without even themselves knowing it, all the fine keys that open the most secret locks. The latter are not to be blamed any more than the former are to be praised, and there are no explanations to be given for these differences, which only bring to light physiological chance and the mystery of instinct.

This girl was among those who know and when, from Mlle. Jeanne Mignard she became Mme. Pierre Romain, she believed not only that she was going to be able, in a general way, to decree existence and organize her future according to the desires of her heart and the will of her mind but also that she could foresee any particular obstacle, circumvent it, and make it serve the permanence of her happiness.

It was there, in this concern for the real, that precisely that romantic imagination appeared which one might have thought was suppressed in her. It was there that the candor of the virgin and the naivete of the child came to play their roles.

*

She had wanted to be an artist, had run to museums, had enrolled in workshops. She had wanted to write, and she had read a lot, had contrived to converse with men of letters. Eventually, she had given up direct production of artwork, and she had limited her ambition to that of wanting to marry an artist.

It was done. She was the wife of a fashionable sculptor who was very busy during the day with official work and busts for the Salon, welcoming invitations, and who was fond of entertaining in his very sumptuous lodgings in the Monceau quarter. Apart from all that, he was intelligent, aware of the somewhat hasty and artificial profession to which he had consented, quite smart and had some concern for things of the mind, amiable—and amorous.

Jeanne was also in love, very much in love, with her husband and also hastily passionate and jealous. Armed with her reading and her memories, relentless in wanting tomorrows similar to her sweet today, the first reform she carried out concerned the female model necessary for the work of Pierre Romain.

How many tales and novels had she read where a model played a considerable role among painters and sculptors—so destructive to the husband's tenderness and the wife's security! It would not be that way in her home, and she wanted to start the way the others finish in those printed stories. Without difficulty she gained, during the sentimental days and evenings of abandonment which follow the wedding, a promise that a foreign women would not cross the threshold of the workshop any longer. And the studio was henceforth intimate and sacred like a religious alcove, since it was she, the legitimate wife, the sovereign of this artist and his art, who came to undress and immobilize herself there on the platform.

The sculptor willingly accepted this interference of a woman in love. He found a kindness and an advantage in this arrangement which made his wife a collaborator at all times, always ready, and superior in grace and word to those whom he formerly employed.

Moreover, he did not tire her by hard work. He used a lot of photographs and engravings, made extensive use of Antiquity and the Renaissance, sought his inspiration in the immense repertoire of the past, as he had been instructed to do during his years at the School of Fine Arts and the Villa Medici. For the rest, he bought casts which he believed represented the truth in his hasty productions. And he asked Madame Romain to pose for but a few moments to obtain a particular attitude, a drapery effect, a harmony of the whole.

She perfectly fulfilled the role she had wanted to play. She posed, dressed and unveiled, standing, lying down, sitting, she consented to all the poses as her husband had consented to all her commands. She recognized herself in the Salon, in the naves where the white statues stand near green plants. She contemplated herself at the Luxembourg Museum, as a deity of Greek mythology, in gardens and squares, as naiads wet with water from a fountain, as a nymph running above the greenery of a lawn. She saw herself rising as Fame, crowning great men at the roundabouts of public squares. She met herself in cemeteries and in provincial cathedrals, as the muse on famous or rich tombs. She played a role in French propaganda, in an exhibition which took place in Saint Petersburg, and she even went away, cast in bronze, to take her place in an enormous commercial and industrial demonstration organized in Chicago.

✳

Years passed—and suddenly their life changed.

A concern came to Pierre Romain. The bourgeois, dependable, satisfied artist was troubled by a desire. He was startled by the sight of a few glories which appeared, rising on the horizon and invading the sky of Art like tranquil suns. The sculptor, admitted as a notable merchant and decorated medalist for the Institute, suddenly saw a great void. He considered his life as it passed, the plateau of his fortieth year reached, and became aware, in a minute of dreadful illumination, of the childish multiplication of his statues, of the emptiness of his artistic conception, of the nothingness of his work.

He stood idle for some time, defeated and undecided. A meditative contraction changed his placid brow, his hair turning slightly silver.

With a little nervousness and melancholy, he told his wife of new work projects and confided to her ambitions and hopes, of which she approved.

We saw him renounce the world, changing his neighborhood domicile, going to live in a house between a courtyard and a garden on a silent road located on the other side of the water. He spent time with his colleagues, the sculptors who led working-class lives, took their meals in the small wine merchants' shops on Boulevard Montparnasse and Boulevard de Vaugirard and who walked their big beards in sad back-and-forths from their studios to the ministry. He frequented the artistic cities, the houses where the numerous workshops are reminiscent of cloister cells and barrack rooms. He listened to the confidences and theories of this one and that one.

And then he returned to his studio, where he tried to become realistic.

His wife continued to approve, until the day when she noticed that a very particular and unexpected ordeal was beginning for her.

Pierre Romain became a realist, narrowly and terribly. He persisted in studying nature, in performing that view. He wanted to see everything and express everything, and change his vague vision of yesteryear into an authoritarian myopia.

His sessions were now prolonged until fatigue. The world was forsaken, official favor withdrawn. A new existence replaced the old one. And it also seemed to Jeanne that another woman was replacing her, taking her place in her husband's work. Yet it was he who worked, and it was she who posed. Where did it come from that there was no longer a trace of Fame, of the Nymph and the Naiad of yesteryear in these creatures that Pierre Romain modeled with such relentlessness?

She did not recognize herself in this stranger without slenderness, with thick attachments, the breasts a little detached from the torso, the belly too apparent.

"I put down what I see," was the answer to the first, timid objections.

And another time, when Jeanne found herself really too fat, her body too abandoned, too without a corset:

"What do you want, my dear, the body is constantly changing. One has to make what one sees."

Decidedly, it was the style. Alas, why did he embrace this style, why didn't he sculpt what he used to see, in the days of brilliant youth. Maybe now he shouldn't sculpt what he saw, and the work would be all the better for it. Life was unbearable if it had to be looked at like this, through a magnifying glass, represented and erected in the public square with all the scars of bygone years, all the blemishes of age.

These flaws were accentuated, and they appeared violent, harshly expressed by these fingers of the artist, once a skillful creator, who had become a ruthless practitioner. Everything was shown to the woman, annoyed at first, then magnified and in pain, everything from small, natural, ignored flaws to the ravages of motherhood. It was a reasoned accounting of her wrinkles, a pitiless inventory of her carnal existence.

✳

She begged Pierre not to take her as a model any more, to go back to the girls of the past. He refused, consented after a violent scene, came back to her, begged her so much that she had to resign herself. It was his own wife that the sculptor wanted to copy. He had found his way through this delicately faded body, that would mature. He was artistically in love with her autumn.

Gently, with a smile, he happened to note that, "all the same, it could be undone." He recalled his old anatomical studies and pointed out faults in the design and modeling of the body of the adored companion of his existence. He loved these faults, it was "so interesting," it was "so fun!" Yes, he found his wife interesting! He showed his studies, his statues, his pieces, to his friends with the big beards, he passionately explained to them what he was looking for, he boasted to them of the sags and folds which, indeed, filled the beards with joy, but which saddened the unfortunate woman, maddened by the idea of her decrepitude. She lived with only one idea in her head: she felt always and everywhere, day and night, at home, outside, the watchful gaze of her obstinately searching husband. Out for a walk, striding in front of him, she felt his gaze weigh on her back in a formidable way.

It all ended with a logical twist. In seeking a violent distraction, in asking life to reassure her of the anxiety that her youth was really over, or that she could no longer be loved, she took a lover. He was a poet; he reassured her only by capturing her in his books through infinitely pretty precautions of language.

THE TUNNEL

(originally published as "Le Tunnel" in *Le Journal*, July 25, 1896)

I don't know if it's a story that I really lived, or just one that I dreamed while traveling. Perhaps it was told to me by an imaginative person. But it has remained in my memory in the form of a story heard a long time ago, and thusly that I transcribe it today, both vaguely and precisely.

I took the train not in the evening, in the hours of drowsiness and nightmare, but at noon, under a brilliant sun. This fact alone would seem at first to exclude any idea, any possibility of hallucination, but this is a preconceived notion that we need to discard. Daylight has its mysteries, like dusk and like night, and the blazing brightness gave rise to an atmosphere in which things are consumed, tremble and evaporate. The vision can become cloudy, and the mind knows the fever and the torpor under that brightness, and the weight of those torrid days when the earth burns in space.

What has slipped my mind completely was the knowledge of my starting point and the purpose of my journey. I think I had left Paris. But by which station? I saw it and did not recognize it, because it did not hold any particular character. I saw an almost empty public waiting hall, with counters, where a few travelers presented themselves, conveyance drivers pushed luggage with a harassed air. I heard the sound of wagons turning on the turntables, the whistles and the steam outlets resonating and vibrating in the skylights. But was I really in Paris? Maybe I was in Bordeaux or in Nantes, in London, in Basle or in Antwerp or somewhere else entirely, where my restless and wandering mood had taken me, perhaps even in some city where I had never been before. I don't know anymore, but that vast and deserted station full of prolonged noises remained in my memory, confused.

The train left, and I still had the very clear feeling that I was alone in it. The few travelers seen at the counters were going to other places at other times, and I could see them wearily standing on the platform, watching the lazy locomotive and the empty carriages move off.

The direction and name of the place I was heading to also escaped me completely. I searched in vain, with anxiety and despair, but I found nothing, absolutely nothing. Yet I still saw the landscapes I had crossed, landscapes buried under a thick solar vapor which seemed to fall from the heavy and terrible star suspended in the middle of the sky. The fields, the woods, the hills, arose slowly, with effort, from a torrid mist traversed by long undulations. The objects were blue, pink, phosphorescent. We crossed rivers of steaming water, blazing cities, sleepy villages smoldering under the ashes.

At a small station, the train stopped. Here again, I heard a bell ringing, I saw a name that I could no longer read, but I distinctly saw the time on a dial: noon.

I also saw a few people waiting for the train to arrive, and among them a man searched everywhere, looking for a space. His gaze searched all the empty carriages, noticed me at my door, and I was amazed to see that he was headed my way, that it is my compartment that he had chosen.

I withdrew, in a rather bad mood. He sat down at an angle, diagonal from me; the train left, and I looked at the newcomer through my half-closed eyelids.

I recognized his face as bestial and intelligent, with rough features, long ears, a predatory jaw, his mouth protruded like a wolf's muzzle, but with thin, perceptive and wary eyes, set so far apart from each other that they looked almost sideways; his eyes were at odds with his other features. An unusual face that interested but also worried me. For I noticed that he was looking at me too, although his eyes seemed to avoid me. I saw a sour expression pass over his face. His mouth clenched, he rubbed his hands together, cracked his knuckles. And suddenly I could no longer see him, his image had disappeared. We entered a tunnel.

This tunnel was of unusual length, and it was not without annoyance that at the sudden plunge into darkness, I learned that the lamp was not lit. Gradually, for an incalculable time, all the stories of attacks and crimes in compartments came to mind. Suddenly, I was amused by the memory of a drawing by Daumier that represented two placid travelers watching each other mutually, at night, in a wagon, with the same expressions of ferocious fury. I jokingly imagined the stranger conjuring the same fanciful thoughts. Then I had the impression that I was traveling with a wild beast who was going to attack me, its mouth gaping open, and engorge me with its fangs. Gently, I looked for my revolver; it was in my suitcase, over my head, and I did not think I had time to locate it and grab the gun. I tried to remember where the alarm bell was fixed, and I still chuckled at the idea that my hand was going to meet, at that beautiful bell, with the feverish hand of the man...

Violently, the daylight returned. It is then that a real terror seized me: the man was no longer there.

After a stupor, I got up, agitated, terrified by what should have reassured me. How... could this... have happened? I shook the doors: they were hermetically closed, the little blue curtains lowered, the panes open. I looked outside; the latches were on. Was it possible that the man had left noiselessly, that he put everything back in place and escaped from this moving train? Looking under the seats, I tried to see into the adjoining compartments through the little triangular panes. Finally, exhausted by worry and breathless curiosity, I pulled on the alarm bell, bringing everything to a halt. The train stopped.

To the clerk who arrived I told, in a hasty and feverish voice, my extraordinary adventure. He looked at me coldly, urged me to end the joke, threatened me with a report. I insisted. I appealed to his memory, asking him if he remembered having closed the door on a man with such and such an appearance, such and such a countenance. He remembered nothing.

I got out, led him along the train, looking everywhere for the stranger with feverish haste. The few travelers, as well as the mechanic and driver, bent their heads impatiently. The employee took me back inside, and with great caution and condescension reassured me, telling me that there would be an investigation as soon as we arrived at the next station. I saw that he took me for a madman.

Despite everything, at the station I jumped out and repeated the whole thing again to the stationmaster, letting my train go, wanting to be clear of all that. Due to my confident air, I was allowed to explore the tracks. I went with a man who carried a lantern, and explored the tunnel where we found nothing, no trace... and beyond that it is impossible for me to remember what happened...

AMBITIOUS

(originally published as "Ambitieuse" in
Le Journal, January 9, 1897)

SHE was the wife of a painter, an exact and fine landscape painter, who rigorously planned and completed his nuanced works as he slowly executed engravings. The meticulousness of his manner did not prevent this honest artist from being ardent and crazy about his profession, dreaming constantly and enthusiastically about nature, about its multiple aspects which delighted him, which intoxicated him. He desired to seize all beautiful and enchanting spectacles, to fix them by drawing and color; but his eyes and his mind were always ready to see them, to rejoice in them, and by thought and word to possess them. He thus lived a happy life, a life adorned, at every moment, with the renewed magic of things.

Most likely this existence of perpetual contemplation prevented the excellent painter from becoming a practical producer. Exhibition halls and merchants' shops interested him much less than anything unfolding under the sky: the curve of a river, the undulating top of a forest, the moving surface of a field of wheat. He liked to ignore everything about social life and to focus only on the beauty of the universe. For a long time his cherished and most intimate project was to flee to some solitude where he could study the shades of the ancient, charming face of the world.

But the flat necessity of living is stronger than the most violent imagination, and the two had to stay in Paris.

It is not possible to live in the country without owning a country house, however small it may be, and to live in this house by the sole aid of work required no less than the supreme disdain and irreducible energy of a Jean-François Millet. This obstacle surmounted, Millet lived on the necessities, and tranquility, and was by no means a wretch. The entire challenge was to overcome the obstacle, and the artist, whose life with his wife is briefly described here, did not know that, or did not dare it by himself.

His wife imposed her idea of life onto him, and he accepted the program and obeyed her orders.

What orders, what program, what idea? The marvelous thing was that it never had a formula, and that the practical desires of the wife remained as vague, infinitely more vague, than the daydreams of the husband.

The wife found things to object to, and her brooding, her silences, her sulks were the unanswerable arguments by which all the hopes and all the chimerical imaginings of her husband were nipped in the bud. The woman may not have known very well what she wanted, but what she didn't want she affirmed with an invincible passive force. She resisted her companion's whims, and these quiet fights resulted in... nothing. The two beings remained where they were, combining their lives together without living them, waiting—they didn't know *why*, he rather philosophical and resigned, she champing at the bit, impatient and sad.

No conjugal catastrophe ensued, nor the perpetual and horrible drama of bad moods with a thousand pretexts, a thousand diverse acts. Only a few speeches, a few attempts at reasoning.

One day when she was complaining once more about the mediocre, stagnant, hopeless life to which she found herself condemned, she confessed to being ambitious and she displayed a painful contraction of her face, which moved the sincere man to whom she was confiding her secret thought. There was a mixture of shame and pride in her at revealing herself like this. Yes, ambitious. She was ambitious. "For what?" the other naively asked.

She would have been hard put to answer that specific detail. Ambitious for what? Well, for everything, and even more! Basically, the whole debate between these two people was summed up in this and their ideas of existence were formulated in the same way. The man had wanted to conquer the whole universe, and so had she. But the difference, however, was that the man had the conscious desire to transpose this universe onto his canvases, in forms and colors, while the woman was at a loss to articulate what use of her own power she could have made. He tightened the terms of the question, tried to guess what she would have liked to add to the average life that was theirs: spacious lodging, a full table, flowers, elegance? All of these can be had without luxury, as part of a material life. Perhaps the decor of a sentimental life: love, children, friendships?

He was elated to enumerate all these joys, rendered profound and complete by art.

To all of it, she said "yes," but still she wasn't convinced. She agreed that the existence of rich people might only be pleasant from a distance, and that the pleasure of having a servant in a black coat behind you during the meal must be a pleasure quickly exhausted. She didn't deny the peaceful joys, she didn't deny the power of art. But, to tell the truth, she also confessed that she remained sad, unhappy—to be forced to love all this, and *only* this, and that she had in her a sad and violent feeling, a kind of incurable annoyance at having no freedom to possess everything. She loved, she said, everything she did not have and she knew how to recognize, with good grace, the absurdity of her wishes, since she knew in advance that she could no longer love what she might obtain: "I'm often angry with you," she said, "for not having accomplished all the thoughts that agitate me, for taking pleasure only in your work, for not thinking of fame, nor of success, nor of money. I blame you, but I know that I'm being unfair, and that I should be happy since you're happy."

She thus admitted to being ambitious without a goal, ambitious without temperament. A woman who wants these destinies creates them, she animates the indolent companion, she charges him with a mission, she persuades him of the importance of *his* role, so that she can play hers; she considers him as a partner who bears the weight of business and urges him, every day, to go to war.

But she was unable to convince her companion of the need for appearances. It was, therefore, up to him to convince her of the superiority of the inner life—because they could not stay in this uncertain region where they have now marked their distances.

THE DISCOVERY
(Originally published as "La Decouverte" in *La Journal*, July 9, 1897)

THE king of fences and outer boulevards, formidably born with unconscious instincts of laziness, battle and murder, certainly that fellow was quite frightening to behold when he strolled his animal beauty indolently along the sidewalks. He had the appearance of a carnivorous beast, alternately low and angry, with supple and strong movements, an air of sniffing out and choosing prey. His face was made of a hound's jaw adorned with a thin black mustache, a hint of a nose, small bright eyes set far apart. His wrestler's build and his elegant villainy had earned him, without question, absolute authority in the region where fate had caused him to be born and live. While young, almost a child, he was already endowed with the strength and skill of an athlete, and had provoked and defeated, in single combat, a formidable guy, a "Terror" venerated for ten years, who was aging into a cowardly softness. After this brilliant action, the newcomer had been proclaimed "Terror" in his turn by his dazzled comrades, and he had lived ever since, reigning over men and women, like a clan chief in the midst of his harem and companions in arms.

He could not conceive of any existence other than that, the violent, savage, hunted existence, with hours of calm and laziness. Randomly born, immediately thrown into the stream, arrested as a vagrant, kept at La Roquette, escaped, returned to the street, he had ambition to owe his food, his home, his pleasures, only to his Herculean strength, and to his pimping grace.

In the off-seasons, he added to his occupations of war and pleasure, and his interludes of strolling, a few enterprises of theft, but his taste was not for simple trickery. He loved to divide his days between fiercely contested battles and rest earned by victory. Theft only smiled on him when there was strategy, violence, armed robbery of some well-guarded cash box, of some passer-by willing and able to defend himself. The young Terror often returned wounded, torn, bruised, from these expeditions as a feudal chief, but always found on his return the adulation and care of his faithful tribe.

The pleasures of this period were, along with love, absinthe and coffee in the bar, a game of cards and a game of billiards, the theater once a week, afternoons spent sleeping in the dry grass of the fortifications, and sometimes a session of fishing or a swim in the canal. But these outings from Paris were rare, and the man did not willingly leave the pavement, the streaming crowd, the zinc bar, the alcohol, the blue wine, the game, the brawl, the open boulevard where his companions come and go.

But he now has another style.

The bicycle exercised a singular, disturbing, civilizing influence on him.

He rented, and he now owns, that precious machine, whether he seized it by cunning or force or whether he owed it to extra work and to the prodigies of economy of his female partners. Immediately, a new passion, that of departure, of speed, of intoxication from the air, awoke and grew in him. He had had no idea what could be seen beyond the fences. From the top of the embankments where he basked in his lazy power, he had never seen anything but roofs and mine pipes, a horizon of stones, bricks and smoke. At the canal, he frolicked in the midst of a teeming humanity, he found the regulars of his bar and his boulevard. And now, suddenly, after a few turns of the wheel, he found himself alone, on a beautiful road, in the middle of the countryside. Tall trees, such as he had never seen, quiver softly, with all their tender green leaves in the golden morning air. From everywhere, branches, furrows, fall and rise the songs and cries of birds. In the meadows colts and fillies run and jump, oxen and cows graze gravely. In the middle of the fields, thatched roofs smoke, silhouettes that lean towards the ground straighten up to watch the traveler pass.

He sees it all very quickly, on the run, feels it more than he understands it. He only notices that he is transported as if by magic, into a new, unsuspected world; he undergoes the caress of the air, a cool caress which relieves the fever of his obtuse alcoholic head. He runs through a pure unaware light. Faster, faster still: he wouldn't want to stop, and he is furious, on returning in the evening, to experience the smoky suburb again, the jolting cobblestones, the stifling street, the black stream, the smell of absinthe.

From now on he continues like this, machine-like and bewildered. He grimaced the first few days, drinking fresh wine from some inn, that season's poor wine that he found clear and sour, eating bread that tasted like flour, the omelet made from the fresh eggs of a chicken coop, smoked bacon from the fireplace, herbs from the garden. But only the countryside offers these remedies for his cravings, and now, in the evening, he finds decomposed and adulterated tastes in the meats and wines of the tavern.

What will become of him, I don't know. Is he going to transport the vices and crimes he lived on into the solitudes, or is this twenty-year-old brute going to be appeased by the breath of space? The other day, an accident happened to his machine, on a road to Normandy, and a cyclist running at full speed stopped without being asked, helped, with a screw, a tool, to repair the damage, the scoundrel had to thank him in his hoarse voice, and had for the first time a vague perception of disinterested benefit and solidarity.

He is thus, changed and uncertain without knowing it, vaguely desirous of another profession than that which he exercises at the crossroads, incapable of judging his marshy existence, but avid of the race, of the light, of the wind. He has become the maniacal lover of his bicycle, he has abandoned the bar counter, he has cured himself of alcohol, he passes the fences without seeing anything, goes off to discover he does not know what, and only comes back to leave.

A GOOD ABSINTHE

(originally published as "La Bonne Absinthe" in *Le Journal*, August 6, 1897)

L AST evening in the heavy heat of the end of the day and the last light of the sun, I had stopped at the bottom of the suburb, at the intersection of the uphill street and the boulevard shaded by plane trees. The crowd flocked to the vast crossroads, rising incessantly from a Paris just glimpsed in the evening mist. The march of all these people, who were returning from their work, had the character of an assault, of a repossession of home, of the place of rest, of strolling, of familiar pleasure. Infinite shades, probably, could be observed in the movements and expressions of all those who thus returned to their lodgings. Fatigue and discouragement were visible in some who remained motionless for a moment, to wheeze like horses being hoisted, at the bottom of a hill. But that evening, among the great number, the marching movement had an aspect of strength and joy. These free paces, these supple and strong men of all appearances and all races, these women with courageous faces, these little girls with slender waists, these garlands of children, everything expressed the joy of living, of owning the street, the trees, the pink sky, the warmth and clarity of summer. However, at this crossroads, there was a stop where this moving force was diminished, where the future was engaged.

Everywhere you turned there was an immense establishment, a new-style bar with its counter, its tables, its distillery apparatus; clean barbaric shops, sparkling with copper, pewter, glass, mirrors where thirst is administratively regulated. The four facades, red and gold, blazed under the rays of the setting sun, the enormous letters and figures displayed their marvelous promises. A boss, perched on a high chair above the massive counter, was the priest and the idol dominating the altar. The rooms had naves and aisles, like churches do, and in one there even stood an organ ready to roar and give rhythm to the services of drink.

The organ, however, was silent, and every hall was empty. The clientele remained outside at the little tables, invading the pavement, an enormous clientele in tight ranks like at the theatre, all the tumult, all the gesticulation, all the laziness and all the bliss too. Everywhere, in all the glasses, absinthe, and the atmosphere fragrant with the violent scent of the forest.

The show, despite everything, kept its sweetness, its charm, its blooming life.

They weren't the gloomy types, the rows of idiots I often observed, standing at the counter or seated on high chairs, not taking their eyes off the bewitching liquor, mechanically stirring the spoon in the murky opal. People here, outside, kept a liveliness, a conversation, a laugh. They knew the point at which to stop. I saw those who had to make a stop slow, stand for a moment on the refuge under the branches of the candelabrum, cast a circular look around them, choose their corner, and go to a table. They were not isolated absinthe maniacs: they were undoubtedly beginning their apprenticeship in poison; they found the flavor charming, the bait delicious.

In groups of friends or family, they sat down. Immediately, the glasses were on the table, and the waiter, with an expert hand, measured oblivion and joy. I sat down, like everyone else, and before I asked anything, an absinthe also appeared in front of me. I then noticed that the drink was served, not in the usual big and tall glasses, but in small stemmed glasses, wine glasses. Taken like this, absinthe seemed to lose its importance: we didn't drink, we tasted, in these little glasses, which were really children's glasses. Simple illusion, moreover, created by the malice of the industrialist. The "small absinthe" is worth the big one, the quantity is the same: you have less water to add, that's all.

But the calculation was a good one, because the nice little stemmed glass attracts, with its pale color and its fine scent, women who would perhaps recoil at first before the huge cup of drink. The women, indeed, were numerous, and all drank their little absinthe, like men. Some had slight hesitations, simpering as if around a forbidden fruit. They advanced their lips, tasting greedily, and their beautiful eyes shone lovingly. Very close to me, a group of good people, three men, two women, were thus seated around pretty absinthes. The women, delicately, pouring the water drop by drop, melted a piece of sugar above the glass. Soon a little girl came to join the group, a barely adolescent girl, beautiful twisted blonde hair, cornflower blue eyes, peach-velvet cheeks, a pink bodice hiding her young breasts.

Like the others, she took an absinthe, and the blue of her eyes was reflected in the little green swamp.

One of the men, at this moment, took the floor, addressing one of the women, explaining to her what a good absinthe was.

"Do you know," he said to her, "how you have to go about it, so that the absinthe doesn't do any harm?"

There was attention. Surely, that would be very valuable, wouldn't it? To be assured of impunity.

"Well!" said this good man, while everyone looked at his beaming face and listened to his friendly words, "Well! My children, this is what must be done. You take a lot, a good half glass. You add the water very slowly, a drop every minute. You have to be patient. Then, well installed in the shade, you watch the passers-by watch *your* mixture. Take an

hour if necessary to properly prepare. And
then…?"

"So ?"

"When it's over, you take your glass and
throw the absinthe down on the floor. You're
sure it won't hurt *you*."

He laughed jovially, drank the end of his
glass: everyone laughed with him at the farce,
and everyone too, the women, the little pink
girl, finished drinking their absinthe with a
happy heart.

FATHER VIPER
(originally published as "Le Pere La Vipere" in *Le Journal*, August 13, 1897)

IN the forest of Fontainebleau, in the jumble of hedges, shrubs, among the stones, around small ponds, the silent and prudent man searches, questioning. He is dressed in a blouse, wearing an old hat and strong boots, a stick in his hand, a box hanging from his neck. Does he want violets or lilies, does he hunt insects, does he collect pebbles or plants? Is he a botanist, an entomologist, a geologist? Suddenly he stops. Through the grass, on a flat stone, in the sun, he has just seen a kind of curved, cylindrical ribbon, adorned with a zig-zag stripe. A midge buzzes by, fleeing with a violent swoop of wings. A double thread wriggles at the end of the ribbon. Sparkling eyes of red and black fire stare at the man. The serpent sees the enemy. The solitary walker is a hunter of vipers.

There is a pause, an immobility of a second. Then, the man takes a step, the viper leaves his stone, flees undulating on the ground. There is a small empty space to cross to reach the sanctuary of shrubs and crevices. It is there that the hunter, with a rapid movement, raising his forked stick at the end, seizes the creature by the neck, which undulates more strongly and struggles on the ground like an eel in the water. Anger animates it, enlarges its flat and vigorous head, its mouth opens, its fangs protrude, it takes on the appearance of a tiger with its flat skull, its short muzzle, its set jaw. While it squirms, the tail curling around the stick, the man places the opening of the box over her. It enters, it is a prisoner.

If the viper escapes, during this rapid struggle, the man rushes forward, crushing its head with a kick of his heel. If it is only hurt, he seizes the stunned animal with his fingers by the neck, tears out its fangs with pliers, and imprisons it. And on to the next one.

This man, for forty years, has been doing this job. In the hot season, every day he goes to the places where he is sure to hear the stealthy glide of the beast in the previous year's dry leaves, where he is sure to see the gleam of the red and black eye and the waving, spotted gray ribbon. He gradually developed a passion for this pursuit and this capture, and he celebrates his hunt for vipers with more gusto than the hunters of harmless hares and partridges. The mystery and the danger exalt him, giving him the subtle senses of a man of yesteryear who lived in the silences and noises of solitude. His keen eyesight distinguishes the reptile's spots among the pebbles, the stones, the foliage, the branches of dead wood, and he also claims that his trained sense of smell can sniff out the animal's slightly fetid odor, through all the scents and the perfumes of the forest.

He began to beat the bushes back when the growing influx of reptiles put a price on each animal taken and killed. Many peasants, day laborers moreover, took part in the hunt to receive the bonus of fifty centimes. Then the price dropped to twenty-five centimes. Many hunters gave up the game. Our lonely man had taken a liking to it, persisted, and his persistence earned him fame: he became Father Viper.

The fact is, he had no other family. He lived alone, in a hut, at the edge of a pine wood. It was there, every day, that he brought back the proceeds of his hunts. He had not been satisfied with the official twenty-five centimes, and had enlarged his circle of customers. The living vipers, which he took in quantity, he kept and fed with worms, insects, toads, frogs, kept them in reserve for natural history museums and laboratory experiments. The vipers that were killed well, not damaged, or which died at home of natural death, were intended for the honors of the jar, to be showcased by pharmacists. A very large number went to remedies, administered by bonesetters and old doctors, the broth of viper being used for chronic diseases, the fat desired by the peasants to cure themselves of poisonous bites, the dried skins hanging on the walls and the beams of the stables to protect animals: cows, sheep, pigs.

Father Viper eats, sleeps, daydreams, and hums in the middle of all these snakes, in his only room on the beaten floor which resembles both a scholar's study and a peasant's bedroom. In the evening, at night, or during his absences, there is no need to lock the door. Passersby do not want to enter, dogs make a detour. This guy lives quietly with his collection, without nightmares. He makes his rounds before going to bed, looks at the little triangular heads, the fierce, hard, sad eyes, always bright, always open, and he falls asleep under the skins that hang from the joists.

All his skill does not prevent him from being bitten quite often. It takes such swiftness to seize the fleeing beast! And then, the old man has acquired too much self-confidence, and naively believes he is safe. When bitten, always on the hands, he does not let go of the animal, finishes it off, breaks its head with his iron heel, and immediately turns to healing himself. With a sharp knife, which cuts like a razor, he carves and removes the flesh around the soft little points that mark where the fangs entered. He lights a handful of matches, stuffs them into the wound, chars the flesh. His fingers are slashed, shapeless, bloody, but Father Viper—free from all fever, all illness, all fear—has not given up his mania, his passion.

He even keeps a young viper who had bitten him in this way. He freed it of its fangs and small teeth, and it lived in freedom at his house, coiled up under a blanket or sliding along the walls, coiled in its basket near the stove during the winter, becoming numb with deep cold. In the spring, it wakes up, stretches, comes to tickle the old man's poor scarred hands with its forked tongue. When he returns from his hunts, at a bend in the path, he whistles and it comes to the threshold and whistles too. He brings it insects or some little beast of the woods. When it strays from the house he is worried, and fears the boor who would kill it for five sous, and so he puts a plate full of milk in front of its door, to which it greedily runs. He laughs and scolds it, removes the plate that the little triangular head hastens to, amused by its disappointment, its frustrated crawling. The reward, at last, for it efforts and determination to follow him, is his return of the milk for its gluttony. On Sundays, he rests, stays at home, puts away his bottles and boxes, makes his labels, writes his notes. When finished, at sunset, he sits down in front of his humble dwelling and calls his favorite. It comes and he plays for it, on an elderberry flute, an air which it listens to, raised on its tail, swinging its head.

JEALOUSY

(originally published as "La Jalouse" in *La Lanterne*, **October 5, 1897)**

Awoman watched the man she loved as he died. She couldn't be mistaken; the awful symptoms appeared making any illusions impossible. The pale face, the thin nose, those cloudy, faintly wandering eyes, the sweaty hair! She took the hand that rested on the sheet, a very cold, very light skeleton of a hand. She spoke, questioning in a soft voice, but no words answered her, the pale head only tried to move, the eyes barely turned.

The abyss of pain deepened in the unhappy woman. She lived that afternoon in a crisis of prostration and revolt, overwhelmed, then furious, falling into stifled sobs of despair, rising in rages of protest, begging the doctor, accusing him, rushing to use life-saving drugs, breaking useless vials, going through all the alternatives of despair and willpower. For a moment, with the idea of ending her life as well, she looked in a drawer to find a weapon ready for death, and immediately she returned to the bed of agony, enraged, wanting to break the spell and save the dying person.

This latter, towards twilight, came out of his torpor and regained his speech.

He wandered a little, stuttered, then the sentences formed. With his eyes, he called his love to his side, very close, and he spoke of varied confidences in a very distant voice, which seemed a voice from beyond the grave to her. Beneath the whispering, the murmur, one felt convulsions, the violent movements of the body ravaged by fever, exalted and disorderly.

"I know I'm going to die," he said, "I know I won't last the night."

She protested, nothing but the pleasant clamor of life in her, and wrapped her arms around him, kissed his mouth, with its already funereal grin. He regained his strength, she could hear that he was asking her for forgiveness, he knew he was hurting her but he didn't want to leave without telling her that he had betrayed her. She guessed, but only shuddered at the thought of the evoked departure, of a death that appeared more visible every minute.

"Silence," she cried, "and don't say you're going to die, you're wrong, you're going to live, I'll save you."

"No," he said, "I'm going to die. Forgive me. I betrayed you, I cheated on you, you whom I loved, you who loved me."

He spoke in the past tense, as if he had already passed away, and the woman's tears as she leaned over him increased and fell on his pale face. In a dull voice, with an exhausted if tenacious will that mumbled out his fixation, he told her the truth that stirred in him. He said that while loving her, he had loved other women; he named them to her, some she knew and others she didn't know, still others whose names he himself didn't know, as he had found them in the street of prostitutes where he would run after leaving her. He finished, repeating again that he wanted the forgiveness of this faithful woman, who had loved him so jealously, so fiercely.

She heard the abominable confidence, but immediately forgot it and chased it from her mind. He must live, all the rest was in vain, all the rest was in the past. He had been guilty, he would no longer be so, a new existence would begin for them, as soon as the illness had gone.

He had fallen back into silence, calm now, a little joy shining deep in his tarnished eyes. She became animated, engaged the battle with more ardor, re-read the prescriptions, remembered the doctor's recommendations, gave the exact treatment. When night came and the lamp was lit, after his last spoonful of potion, the patient seemed to fall into nothingness. She was frightened, called to him, touched the wrist, the temple, the heart, held the mirror to his lips, to check for breath. He was alive, but sleeping.

All night she watched him, anxious. Several times he opened his eyes, asked for a drink, and always returned to sleep. In the morning, when dawn came, he was calm and it seemed to the woman that a little of the warmth of life had returned, replacing the fire and the ice of the fever. He lived—after long days and weeks when it was uncertain whether he was going to capsize forever or regain the fragile balance of existence. He lived, and it was she, admirable in care and devotion, who gave him life.

Day by day, she watched him reborn, she saw the faint color rising in his face, his faded eyes blooming again, she heard his voice, already buried in the grave, returning. He no longer knew the delirium of those days of agony; several times he wanted to speak again, his eyes imploring, his voice becoming repentant. She stopped him from proceeding, gave her hand to be kissed by his mute mouth.

It was soon time for recovery. The lover felt triumph to see, standing alongside her and approaching the window while inhaling the air from the garden, the one she had fought for and snatched from death.

For a long time he stayed in the room where love and death had tragically cohabited. He knew the days of calm, the silent nights when one feels protected by an ardent and devoted being. With his strength restored, he was able to descend, leaning on the arm of his dear companion, and walk through the rows of roses, breathe in the heat and the shade, sit down in front of the house. Finally, still with her, he walked outside, into the road; he was once again a man who was master of his world.

The next day, in the morning, with the joy of his rediscovered youth and his remade life, he departed alone, following a full embrace, and bidding goodbye in a full voice. She also said goodbye, in a happy voice. He closed the door. She shuddered. He went down the stairs. She ran to the window, she saw him in the garden, intoxicated by the place he was going to walk through, handsome, young, radiant, alive.

A tear filled her eye. She saw he was ready for betrayal. With a bound she went to the drawer, grabbed the weapon, came back.

He picked a rose, his face lighting up with a mysterious smile.

She aimed the gun and killed him.

THE WOLF

(originally published as "Le Loup" in *La Lanterne*, January 23, 1900)

PIERRE fell in love with Françoise. He was young, strong, a hard worker and of a peaceful and obstinate character. When he embraced and pegged to the bottom of his soul, the idea that this one and not another should be his, his fate was decided. He realized and instinctually sensed in this Françoise, a being similar to himself, placid and obstinate. Their eyes had met and their hearts understood.

One evening, while returning from the fields, the young man met the young girl. He told her, in rather slow and embarrassed words, that he wanted her for his wife. She replied that she wanted this as well. For a moment, in silence, they inhaled the delicate scent of new hawthorn. Then Pierre announced that the next day, which was a Sunday, he would go and declare himself to Françoise's father and mother. She said again that she agreed but her face darkened, as if suddenly, despite the clear sky, a black cloud was passing above them. Pierre understood, remembering his Françoise's terrible father, the farmer Jean Blocqueville, who was called the Wolf.

The Wolf was the name by which he was known for ten leagues around. Without knowing exactly what he was capable of, the instinct of his neighbors and the fear felt by the children and women made Jean Blocqueville thought of as a formidable carnivore, crouched in his house as if in a den, wandering his land anxiously and wildly, hiding behind hedges and in the corners of the woods.

He was a hard-working man, living only for the land in his isolated farm, in the middle of large expanses of fields and plowed land. The ceaseless work should have soothed his fierce temper. Going to bed at seven o'clock and getting up at dawn after nine hours of restorative sleep, he again rushed into the furrows, watching, working, plowing, digging, weeding. He saw only the earth, defeated and absorbed by it in his daily battle. A love of money, the greedy desire of the exploited field, of the wheat that one sells, of the bag that rings, that bitter and inexorable interest alone governed his charred brain. He constantly pursues the heavy crown, grabs it with his greedy hands, adds it to the pile with the others, changes it into gold or paper taken carefully to the notary, finally converts it into fields, into wood, in small holdings.

But for everything else, only mistrust and cruelty. Hard on people, hard on animals—although not animals that have cost him money and represent the money to come, but those he regards as harmful or simply useless. For those animals who do not work, who cross the field or who sing in the trees, there is no mercy, and sometimes even fierce fire. The Wolf has often been seen plucking alive the chicks found in the mown meadows, and martyring the toads which leap heavily in the evening, on the trails.

Pierre, the day laborer who has not a penny, not a furrow of earth, who has only his arms to work, only his youth to exploit, must go to this man, who is brutal and rich. His fear and worry are shared! Françoise wants him as a man, despite his poverty, despite her own dowry, and her father's property, and the terrible temper of the dreaded master. Their love is an idyll in the fields, they are fearful lovers, gentle and hopeful, shy and pensive. But the Wolf is not of this species, and another reality comes into play with him.

He is amused by the request made to him, he laughs at it with bared gums, showing his sharp, white teeth. He soon chases Pierre away, pushes him to the threshold, where the Wolf remains standing, showing a rough and sardonic face, which signifies defense and threat.

However, Pierre returned. He didn't come back by day, he came back by night. At the hours when the dogs and the roosters were sleeping, the country Romeo entered through the window, and the eternal human duet began again in a room as hostile and dangerous as the room of the lovers in Verona. Françoise became Pierre's mistress and gave birth to a stillborn child, to the great anger of the Wolf, who more furiously than ever refused the marriage. He even sought out a husband for his daughter, who might overlook the stupid love affair, the pregnancy, the dead child. It was not difficult, since acceptance came with a respectable bag of money. A local boy, also rich, eagerly agreed to become Françoise's fiancé and husband, and Françoise, beaten by her father, finally consented to the marriage.

But she housed pain and resentment in her soul, in her village woman's soul. She continued, before the nuptial ceremony, to receive Pierre in her room, despite warnings and surveillance. Her two little brothers were made to sleep in the same room, and her cousin Annette, a young girl of eighteen, in the same bed. This Annette, who saw and heard the lovers with little difficulty, warned Jean Blocqueville, the Wolf.

Father Wolf, Mother Wolf, and a Cub son burst into the room, the father armed with a revolver, the mother with a club, the son holding a candle. Pierre was pulled out of the hiding place where he huddled. The revolver shot missed, but the Wolf's claws strangle Pierre, the staff knocks him out, fists and feet crush him.

The cunning murderers then called the neighbors, putting themselves under the protection of the law. A man broke into their home, at night, like a thief! They defended themselves, and they killed him, what could be simpler!

"Look," Jean Blocqueville said to the neighbors, still squatting on his victim, "look at this handsome fellow who has put himself in the mouth of the wolf. He won't be coming back anytime soon, because I'm sure he's dead."

And to another neighbor:

"Look at this pretty rabbit we took. Here he is, he won't frolic anymore."

And the mother struck the cracked skull again with her cudgel, and Father Wolf kept choking the man he had already strangled once.

THE RACER
(originally published as "Le Chauffeur" in
La Lanterne, December 6, 1900)

When a motor car made its appearance for the first time in the village of X, the astonishment was great. We had seen a few bicycles pass, and suddenly the slight machine, almost silent, showing its soft curves and rapid movements, appeared and disappeared in an instant on the road, arousing astonishment and emotion. The peasants in their fields, the shopkeepers on their doorsteps, the petty bourgeois at their windows, had remained for a moment bewildered by the passage of these machines that carried human beings, machines which changed all established ideas about speed and distance. But it was a real anxiety that took hold of the peaceful population at the appearance of the automobile.

When the cloud of dust took shape in the distance, rolled, grew, and a shrill rumble was heard, those who had traveled a little, whose business had brought them to the station located twelve leagues from the village of X, had the mad thought that an accident had occurred, that a locomotive had escaped and that it descended the hill with a furious movement, to knock down walls and tear open the houses, crushing everything in its path. Hadn't we recently read that one of these frightful machines had punched through the facade of a station in Paris and thrown itself into the square, crushing a newsstand and the shopkeeper? So, there was nothing implausible in this belief of a reckless, racing train. A few people took refuge at the bottom of the gardens.

Contrary to general expectation, no accident occurred. Those who had not left their observation post, threshold or window, saw the distant image gradually becoming clearer. The thing was a carriage which arrived at full speed, a carriage without a horse where before only the mail courier ever passed at gallop on his lean and courageous horses, the country carts at the regular trot of the good mare, the

140

cabriolet of the doctor always in a hurry. But what were these gallops, these trots, these active gaits worth, in comparison with this dazzling object moving up the road? We wouldn't even have had time to catch a glimpse of the singular object advancing at such a thunderous rate, if it hadn't visibly slowed its course on arriving at the first houses of the village.

We then saw, still running at a good pace, this strange device: very low between its four wheels, with a whole engine at the back, shiny handles at the front and a flared orifice from which came a trumpet call. There were two tiny seats with backrests, one behind the other. The first alone was occupied by an extraordinary character. Wrapped in a high-collared overcoat, wearing an immense round cap whose visor protected him like a canopy, his eyes locked under goggles with thick lenses and black mesh, similar to the goggles of the road-mender who broke pebbles a stone's throw away. From here, you could only see the tip of his nose, a beard, gloved hands leaning on the handles, booted feet fixed to the pedals. The individual, covered in dust, was as white as the road.

He stopped his hectic machine short, in front of the Auberge de la Croix-Blanche, jumped off fantastic and mysterious, and ordered his lunch from the terrified hostess, returned to his iron beast around which a circle of on-lookers was beginning to form. The dogs had come first, strollers and scenters. Then, the children, leaving the street games, then the shopkeepers, detached from their thresholds. Some bourgeois could not resist the invitation to observe and discuss; among them a graceful woman, looking a little weary and bored, with bold eyes, and her husband, of important bearing.

This latter questioned the motorist who accepted questions just enough to provide some information in a curt voice, indicating the various parts whose use he explained. He ended the dialogue by asking for the wheel-wright's address, and was directed to the bottom of the hill. It was a minor repair and the stranger thought he had time to go and come back while his meal was being prepared. Put back into place, a few strokes of the piston, a few turns of the wheel and he leaves, to soon return again among the amazed population.

He hears, on his return, the end of the conversation between husband and wife: "Certainly," said the large man, "the gentleman would have consented to take you with him, to give you an idea of the speed."

"Certainly yes," replied the mechanic, darting a glint of his goggles at the couple, "and if you don't mind, I'll be at your disposal presently."

They greeted each other.

Without further explanations the woman, rosy with pleasure, returned soon, her hair solidly coiffed, adorned with a floating green veil and wrapped in a cloak. The husband began a speech, quickly interrupted by a violent warning. The group moved away. The automobile set off at a furious pace, and we could still catch a glimpse of the shivering silhouette of the passenger, the rigid attitude and the sarcastic face of the driver.

The car descended the slope at full speed and then up the opposite slope. We soon saw it at the top of the hill, where we could make out the green veil waving wildly in the breeze of the race, then they disappeared, as if the machine had fallen into an abyss. There was nothing left to do but wait for the return of the pedestrian.

She never came back.

A PARTIAL LIST OF SNUGGLY BOOKS